Strange Stories
of Alaska and the Yukon

Strange Stories
of Alaska and the Yukon

Ed Ferrell

Epicenter Press
Fairbanks/Seattle

Editor: Christine Ummel
Cover design: Elizabeth Watson
Inside design: Sue Mattson
Map: Rusty Nelson
Proofreader: Lois Kelly
Printer: Best Books Manufacturing
Front cover: Background photo: Copyright 1996 Gary Schultz / Alaska Stock Images. Historic photos (from left to right): Courtesy of Alaska State Library/ Clyda Schott Greely collection / PCA 66-612; Courtesy of Alaska State Library / John E. Worden collection / PCA 248-7; Courtesy of Alaska State Library / Skinner collection / PCA 44-3-15.
Interior photos: Page 34, Courtesy of Alaska State Library / C. L. Andrews collection / PCA 45-700. Page 66, Courtesy of Alaska State Library/ Wickersham collection / PCA 277-18-99. Page 90, Courtesy of Alaska State Library / Skinner collection / PCA 44-3-15.

Library of Congress Cataloging-in-Publication Data

Ferrell, Ed.
    Strange Stories of Alaska and the Yukon / by Ed Ferrell.
        p.   cm.
    Includes index.
    ISBN 0-945397-51-8 (pbk.)
    1. Legends--Alaska. 2. Legends--Yukon Territory. 3. Curiosities and wonders--Alaska. 4. Curiosities and wonders--Yukon Territory.
I. Title.
GR110.A4F47 1996
398.2'09798--dc20   96.5220
                                                              CIP

To order STRANGE STORIES OF ALASKA AND THE YUKON, mail $13.95 (Washington residents add $1.14 sales tax) plus $4.00 for shipping to: Epicenter Press, Box 82368, Kenmore, WA 98028.

Booksellers: Retail discounts are available from our trade distributor, Graphic Arts Center Publishing™, Box 10306, Portland, OR 97210. Phone 800-452-3032.

10 9 8 7 6 5 4
Printed in Canada

To my wife, Nancy Ferrell,
an author in her own right,
for her support of my various writing projects,
and to those Alaskan and Canadian pioneers
who recorded their encounters with the unknown.

Contents

Introduction 9
Maps 12

Unknown Creatures 15
The Beast in the Glacier 16
Jacko, the Sasquatch Boy 19
Sea Serpent Encounter 23
Creature from the Depths 26
The Attack of the Sea Cobra 28
Death of a Sea Serpent 32

Strange Inhabitants 35
The Storm Master 36
Mystic Fire-Eater 38
Pygmies of the North Pole 41
The Tail Men 43

Places of Mystery 47
The Valley of Eden 48
Winter in Paradise 51
Where the Waters Run Warm 53
An Oasis in the Arctic 55
Miraculous Mirage 58
The Silent City 61
A Petrified Forest 63

Messengers from Beyond 67
The Ghostly Princess of Baranof's Castle 68
Phantom Footsteps 72
The Last Voyage of the Eliza Anderson 74
Guided by a Ghost...78
The Golden Vision of Anvil Creek 81
Warning on Tagish Lake 85
The Searching Maiden of Tiekel City 87

Contents

Lost Mines 91

The Golden Bar 92

Map to Crescent Lake 94

The Lost Rocker 97

Mountain of Fire 99

The Valley of Gold 104

A Creek Lined with Gold 107

The Haunted Mine 110

Forgotten Civilizations 115

A City of Ice 116

The Coin of Mystery 120

The Aztec Connection 122

Ancient Mine Shaft 124

From the Dawn of Time 126

Lost Tribe of the Arctic 129

Giants of the Past 133

The Mastodon Hunters 134

Tracks of the Mammoth 137

Frozen in Time 138

Entombed in a Glacier 143

The Hunter's Story 145

Killing of the Mammoth 147

Index 156

About the Author 159

Introduction

Several years ago, I was researching the newspaper collection of the Alaska State Library for information on Alaska pioneers. Along with the biographical material I needed, I also found a number of news accounts describing strange and inexplicable events.

At first I passed these stories off as prospector yarns, told over a fifth of bourbon in some mining camp saloon. But when missionaries, territorial officials, and other well-known figures in Canada and Alaska reported similar experiences, I began to take the accounts seriously.

There were men of the cloth like Sheldon Jackson, founder of the Presbyterian Church in Alaska. He told of an incredible discovery of the Pleistocene Age. Territorial Fish Commissioner A. J. Sprague reported contact with a sea serpent. I never knew Mr. Sprague, but Captain Tom Smith, the other witness to that encounter, lived in the Juneau Hotel, a few blocks from my house. Another territorial official of the gold rush era was Lafe Spray. He described a supernatural encounter with ghosts and gold nuggets that occurred in Nome, Alaska, while he was working for the Pioneer Mining Company.

Lost mine stories were common on the American frontier, but only a few were documented. Calvin Barkdull recounted a story at a meeting of the Alaska-Yukon Pioneers in 1936. It was the classic lost mine story, in which a dying prospector gave his doctor a map to a fabulously rich mine. However, this story had a difference: It appeared to be true! The doctor lived in Wrangell, Alaska,

Introduction

where he practiced medicine. His name was Stanton, and he owned a gold deposit receipt for $5,000, which the prospector had given him. Dr. Stanton had gone into partnership with Calvin Barkdull, who then spent years searching for the lost placer mine.

Another lost mine story was documented by Charlie McLode, a prospector in the Wrangell-Cassiar country. The account of how the McLode brothers found a rich placer, previously worked by Alaska Natives, is a story of gold, murder, and revenge.

Among the most fascinating stories published in early northern newspapers and magazines were accounts of artifacts uncovered during mining operations. These relics were dated from pre–Ice Age or earlier periods. One discovery made by the Solomon Mining Company of Nome may have predated the earliest known civilization. Many of these artifacts were examined by scientists and archaeologists. Physical evidence of an unknown prehistoric race, for example, was discovered near Barrow in 1920 by an expedition from the University of Pennsylvania.

In compiling this collection, I have read more than one hundred reels of newspaper microfilm. I have no reservations about the quality of early Alaskan and Canadian publications. As a group, these newspapers and magazines reflected a high degree of professionalism. The editors were generally well-educated; several had law degrees. If the veracity of a story was in question, the editor often expressed his doubts in editorial comments. Apparently, journalists of those days were as concerned with truth and accuracy as their modern counterparts.

Another fact adds credence to the selections included in this book. These news stories were not unique to the Northland; they were part of a frontier phenomenon. Newspapers of the earlier American and Canadian frontiers also carried stories of archaeological discoveries and strange creatures. This suggests to me that artifacts of unknown civilizations and remnants of ancient species survived to relatively modern times. As North America has been settled and developed, these sites and species have been destroyed.

In *Strange Stories of Alaska and the Yukon*, I have compiled forty-three stories of the unknown and the inexplicable. They are lifted directly from the pages of northern newspapers and magazines from the 1880s to the 1940s. Some have been slightly edited to update the spelling and grammar, or to quicken the pace of the story, but otherwise these are the exact words of reporters and witnesses to extraordinary events of the past. I hope you will find these stories as fascinating as I did.

Ed Ferrell
Juneau, Alaska

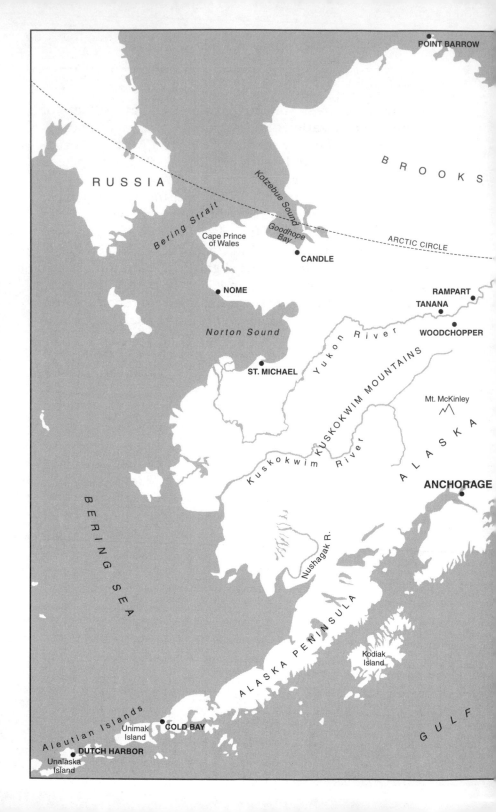

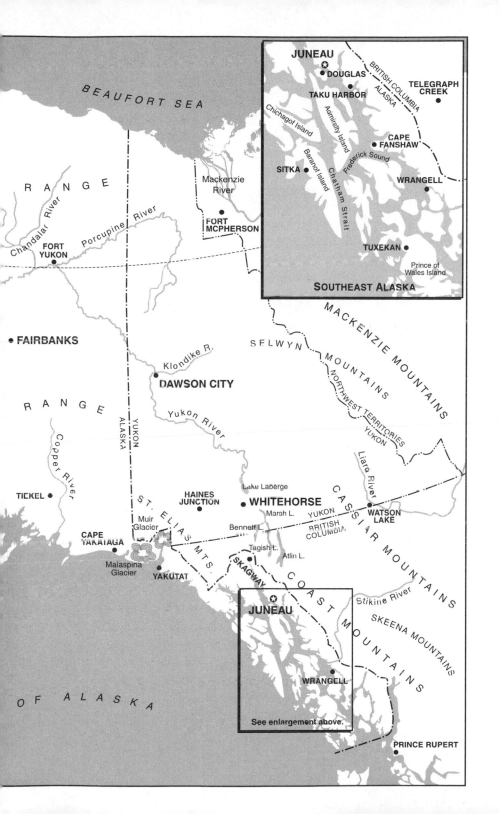

Unknown Creatures

During the gold rush era, stampeders pushed into a great wilderness as large as the present United States, lands we now call Alaska and the Yukon. In this unexplored region, prospectors reported discoveries of creatures unknown to science. Most of these sightings went unrecorded and became part of the oral history of the North Country, but a few encounters were reported in early newspapers and magazines.

Many accounts tell of humanoid species. In Southeast Alaska, the Tlingits told of a man-beast they called "Kosh da kaa." In 1884, the Sasquatch moved out of the realm of legend and became a fact, according to a story in the Victoria Colonist. The British Columbia newspaper reported the capture of a young Sasquatch in Yale, a mining camp in southwestern Canada.

Other tales of unknown creatures take place not on land, but at sea. Many people have reported seeing sea serpents in northern coastal waters, and some have given detailed descriptions of them. The most spectacular evidence of the existence of sea monsters has appeared rather recently — it was recorded by sonar by the fishing boat Mylark off Kodiak Island in 1969. The machine printed out a silhouette of a dinosaur-like creature, estimated to be from 150 to 180 feet in length.

All these stories serve as reminders that much of the Northland is still unexplored. In this wilderness of land and ocean, unknown species may yet be discovered.

Located in the St. Elias Mountains near Yakutat, the Malaspina Glacier covers nearly a thousand square miles. The St. Elias Range is still largely unexplored and could contain an unknown species of humanoid as described by Frank Howard in the March 1909 issue of the Alaska-Yukon Magazine. Mr. Howard's account has been edited for a faster pace, but the narrative is essentially as written.

The Beast in the Glacier

On one of my prospecting trips in Alaska, I met with an adventure that stayed with me all my life. This experience that I am about to relate occurred in Yakutat Bay.

From my camp near the extreme head of the bay, I could look out across one arm of the Malaspina Glacier to a barren rocky ridge. Even at a distance of three miles the ridge showed very perceptible mineral colorings, a mountain of wealth to the eye of the prospector, so I determined to prospect the ridge.

I paddled my canoe along the base of the glacier up to the extreme head of the bay. The face of the glacier was cracked with crevasses which split it from base to brink. Some of the cracks were quite narrow, with sloping benchy bottoms that seemed to offer passable stairways to the top. I selected a narrow crevasse, and with ice-creepers on my boots and pick in hand, I started up. By cutting niches and sinking my ice-creepers deep, in the course of an hour I reached the brink of the great ice plateau and immediately struck across toward the rock ridge. I had expected to find the glacier crevassed, but not such a confusion of chasms as lay before me, for I was looking out over the most broken stretch of glacier I had ever attempted to cross.

As I continued on, with each step the surface grew more broken and the danger increased, until I found myself clinging to the face of an unusually abrupt bench, unable to climb higher.

I raised one foot slightly, but the movement was sufficient to break my hold and I fell into space.

After what seemed an eternity, I landed with a thud, sitting crosswise in a narrow crevasse and wedged down just as tight as the bulk of my body would allow. The impact with the solid ice was a shock that went up my back and nearly lifted my head from my shoulders.

With much difficulty and pain I worked my body up out of the narrow fissure, to a ledge where I sat dazed for several minutes. After I regained my senses, I tried to determine my situation. I tore a leaf from my notebook, lit it, and let it drop into the darkness. It blazed up a moment and revealed bare ground and a safe descent.

I arose and felt my way down the slope with the idea of reaching the water and following along its margin while the tide was low, in search of some crevasse running out to the open bay.

As I kept going ahead I noticed a gradual increase of light. In a few more steps, I stood in a broad wall of hazy blue light that filtered down from above. Looking up, I saw there was no clear opening to the surface, but objects were now revealed some distance around.

Then, to my terror, a form slowly rose out of the glimmer, and took shape. It grew into a spectral thing, a Goliath in the shape of man. But it was malformed in the smallness of the head, the narrowness of the shoulders, and the abnormal breadth of hips. It growled a challenge.

I stood rooted to the spot, the hair raising on the back of my neck. I was engulfed with a rank, indescribable odor. Dazed and terror-stricken, I looked around desperately for a way to escape. But I could not move.

The creature studied me. Apparently satisfied, it walked around me. Before disappearing, the thing turned and again looked at me. Then, watching me with a slantwise glance, it walked obliquely from me until its form faded in the gloom of the cavern.

For many minutes I stared blankly into the darkness, vaguely wondering if the thing would return. In all my years in the northwest wilderness, I had never before seen anything like that.

Dazed and wonder-stricken, I looked around. Below me not fifty feet away, I saw daylight. I walked toward the light, and found an open pathway clear to the timbered bench.

Since my miraculous encounter and escape, I often attempt to solve the mystery that still enshrouds the apparition of the glacier. Terror might have magnified my imagination. But the apparition was not the imagining of an over-balanced mind. I am thoroughly convinced I saw something. It was not like any animal that I had ever seen before.

There is no further record of Frank Howard. Yet his account of the creature he encountered in the glacier is consistent with other reports of Big Foot or Sasquatch.

Despite thousands of sightings, plaster casts of giant footprints, and samples of chimpanzee-like hair, skeptics still dismiss Sasquatch as a myth or hoax. The most damaging argument against the existence of an unknown humanoid is that no one has ever captured one.

According to one newspaper account, however, a Sasquatch was captured in Yale, British Columbia, in 1884. This story was printed in the July 4, 1884, issue of the Victoria Colonist.

Jacko, the Sasquatch Boy

In the immediate vicinity of No. 4 tunnel, situated some twenty miles above this village, are bluffs of rock which have hitherto been insurmountable, but on Monday morning last were successfully scaled by Mr. Onderdon's employees on the regular train from Lytton. Assisted by Mr. Costerton, the British Columbia Express Company's messenger, and a number of men from Lytton and points east of that place, they, after considerable trouble and perilous climbing, succeeded in capturing a creature which may truly be called half man and half beast.

"Jacko," as the creature has been called by his capturers, is something of the gorilla type, standing about four feet, seven inches in height and weighing 127 pounds. He has long, black, strong hair and resembles a human being with one exception: his entire body, excepting his hands (or paws) and feet, is covered with glossy hair about one inch long. His forearm is much longer than a man's forearm, and he possesses extraordinary strength, as he will take hold of a stick and break it by wrenching it or twisting it, which no man living could break in the same way.

Since his capture he is very reticent, only occasionally uttering a noise which is half bark and half growl. He is, however, becoming daily more attached to his keeper, Mr. George Tilbury, of this place, who proposes shortly starting for London, England, to exhibit him.

His favorite food so far is berries, and he drinks fresh milk with evident relish. By advice of Dr. Hannington raw meats have been withheld from Jacko, as the doctor thinks it would have a tendency to make him savage.

The mode of capture was as follows: Ned Austin, the engineer, on coming in sight of the bluff at the eastern end of the No. 4 tunnel, saw what he supposed to be a man lying asleep in close proximity to the track, and as quick as thought blew the signal to apply the brakes. The brakes were instantly applied, and in a few seconds the train was brought to a standstill.

At this moment the supposed man sprang up and, uttering a sharp quick bark, began to climb the steep bluff.

Conductor R. J. Craig and express messenger Costerton, followed by the baggagemen and brakemen, jumped from the train and knowing they were some twenty minutes ahead of time immediately gave chase.

After five minutes of perilous climbing the then-supposed demented Indian was corralled on a projecting shelf of rock where he could neither ascend nor descend.

The query now was how to capture him alive, which was quickly decided by Mr. Craig, who crawled on his hands and knees until he was about forty feet above the creature. Taking a small piece of loose rock he let it fall and it had the desired effect of rendering poor Jacko incapable of resistance for a time at least.

The bell rope was then brought up and Jacko was now lowered to terra firma. After firmly binding him and placing him in the baggage car, "off brakes" was sounded and the train started for Yale. At the station a large crowd who had heard of the capture by telephone from Spuzzum Flat were assembled, each one anxious to have first look at the monstrosity, but they were disappointed, as Jacko had been taken off at the machine shops and placed in charge of his present keeper.

The question naturally arises how came the creature where it was first seen by Mr. Austin. From bruises about its head and body, and apparent soreness since its capture, it is supposed that Jacko ventured too near the edge of the bluff, slipped, fell, and lay where found until the sound of the rushing train aroused him.

Mr. Thomas White and Mr. Gouin, C. E., as well as Mr. Major, who kept a small store about half a mile west of the tunnel during the past two years, have mentioned having seen a curious creature at different points between Camps 13 and 17, but no attention was paid to their remarks as people came to the conclusion that they had seen either a bear or a stray Indian dog.

Who can unravel the mystery that now

surrounds Jacko? Does he belong to a species hitherto unknown in this part of the continent?

Apparently the Colonist *had no additional information on the humanoid, because the editor speculated that the animal had died en route to England.*

Shortly before he died, Knygg Johansen of Wrangell, Alaska, described a sea serpent that he sighted in the Bering Sea in the fall of 1900. For forty-four years, Johansen refused to discuss his sighting until he was interviewed by the Wrangell Sentinel *in 1944. He explained, "I told the story once, and the person I told it to laughed at me and I have never told it again. But I haven't long to live now and it was such a strange thing that I feel it would be wrong to take the knowledge of it to the grave." His account first appeared in the* Wrangell Sentinel *and was reprinted in* Alaska Life *magazine in September of 1944.*

Sea Serpent Encounter

In the year of 1900, I was working for an Alaskan fish canning company on the Nushagak River in Alaska. We had finished our pack on August first and I was put aboard a small steamer as deckhand for our trip to our home port, which was Astoria, Oregon.

At midnight on the tide we left the harbor and after steaming six or seven hours, we were about eighty nautical miles in the Bering Sea. At 8 a.m. it was my turn at the wheel and after having had my breakfast, I went to relieve the other man. He and the captain left for the galley to have their breakfast, which left me alone in the wheelhouse.

The weather was absolutely the finest you could imagine, bright sunshine, no wind — not a ripple on the water.

At this time while looking out across the water, I perceived about 150 feet off the port bow a large animal or fish partially submerged, floating on the water. It was an unusual sight and at that time impressed me so greatly that its every feature is indelibly imprinted on my mind.

I will now describe it as I saw it on that perfectly clear day. I judged the animal or fish to be about twenty-five feet long and about fifteen inches in diameter at the largest part. The main body was the color of kelp, and the tail was a little lighter shade than the rest of the body. The mane was darker than either. The head was out of the water and the tail, or the end of the body, was entirely out of the water when I first saw it. The forehead protruded greatly from the lower part of the face. The eyes were jet black and big and round. From the eyes down the face was more the shape of the faces of cattle, but from the eyes up and back, the face was the exact shape of a horse's face. I could not see how far down the body the mane reached.

The end of the fish or animal was above the water about five feet. This end was a little smaller in diameter than the rest of the body, but not much smaller. There was nothing such as fins, legs, or feet, appended to this part of the body.

In a little while, through movement, other parts of the body became visible. I hollered for someone to come up and observe the object, but it was visible above the water for about half a minute. The tail sank below the water first and the middle of the body came out so that I could see between the ocean and the middle part of the body. This part was about ten feet long. There were no fins, feet, or any apparent means of locomotion.

As we got closer diagonally to the fish or animal, it started to sink. The middle of the body went down. Then the head rose so I could see more of it than I had at first. I could not see any nostrils. The whole animal then sank smoothly. There was not a ripple on the water. The last to disappear was the end of the tail, then the snout — then all was calm.

About that time the skipper came up and wanted to know what I was hollering about. I knew that it was of no avail as there was no way to prove what I had seen, so I said, "Oh nothing; just something I saw."

The sight was so strange and clear that it seems best that I record it. I am getting along in years now and feel that I should let some institution know of my experience so that from my description of its shape and color, a drawing could be made of the fish or animal so that people could understand it and visualize what I saw.

Although not as detailed as Johansen's sighting, Frank Reed's experience was equally amazing. This account was printed in the September 1944 issue of Alaska Life *magazine, under the byline of Genevieve Mayberry.*

Creature from the Depths

Frank Reed had spent many years at sea on sailing vessels and had seen many strange sea animals, but he had never seen anything before or since that compared with the creature he saw in Southeastern Alaska several summers ago.

At that time, Mr. Reed was watchman on a fish trap and lived in a shack on the beach. On this particular day, he was working on his boat, anchored somewhat down from the trap. He heard an unusual amount of splashing, but thought it was the fish trying to escape the trap. The noise was so persistent that Reed turned toward the trap and was astounded to see the most amazing sea creature that he had ever seen. It was tearing at the trap netting with long curved claws. He watched the creature for several minutes, long enough to get a detailed image in his mind.

The thing had a round head approximately the size of a human head which it held stiffly erect as it tore at the netting. The neck was about the same proportions to the head. The "shoulders" were narrower than the shoulders of a man, and the body tapered down to a serpent-like tail. The arms were about the size of the arms of a large man and ended in claws approximately four or five inches long.

Suddenly the creature sighted Reed. It loosed its hold on the net and dropped instantly into the water. Then the most astounding thing happened. The sea creature surfaced a few feet from the trap and swam away at a very rapid rate. It did not swim nor dart like a fish, but made long, powerful, overhead strokes with those powerful arms much like a swimmer.

Frank Reed never saw the gorgonian creature again. He said he regretted ever since that he did not take a picture of the thing as it tore at the fish trap, but he was so dumbfounded that it didn't occur to him until after the creature disappeared.

The June 25, 1894, issue of the Juneau City Mining Record *carried the following story, related by Deputy Marshal Jack Ross and S. A. Keller, both of Douglas City. The paper described them as "two young men of more than average intelligence and reliability." The* Miner's *editor commented: " . . . every now and then persons of more or less credibility report personal sights of such animals and in the main their descriptions agree."*

The Attack of the Sea Cobra

Here is the story as related by these two daring hunters: "When we had reached a spot nearly across the mouth of Lossen Creek which flows into Gastineau Channel," began Jack Ross, "Mr. Keller expressed a desire to go ashore and look up some old landmarks that he had established on a former pedestrian cruise around the island.

"Keller was about to go ashore when he espied two large eagles perched upon a hemlock tree nearby. He instantly seized his rifle and shotgun and started in pursuit of them, but he had no sooner set his foot on shore when his attention was attracted by an unusual noise and on looking around a sight met his eyes that paralyzed him and caused him to drop his weapons."

"On my port quarter," continued Keller, "about three quarters of a mile distant, there loomed the swaying neck and head of some monster unlike anything I had ever seen or dreamed of in all my life, and I have had some terrible experiences. With its head more than ten feet in the air, the monster was swimming directly toward us with fearful velocity, while the mighty throes of his extended body emitted a sound not unlike that caused by the pounding of a side-wheel steamer's paddle.

"My first impulse after regaining my self-control," continued Mr. Keller, "was to reach for my shotgun, but in my excitement, I had strayed some twenty yards from where I had dropped my arms. . . . I had miscalculated the speed of the great serpent. While some distance from my gun, I heard a howl of agony from Jack, and looking over my shoulder, I instinctively fetched a shriek of horror and despair.

"While I was going less than twenty feet, the monster had glided up and pounced upon Jack. Now Jack, as you know, weighs fully 150 pounds and this green-eyed captor was holding him in his mouth more than twenty feet in the air.

"I don't know how I reached the gun, but in less time than it takes to record it, I had seized the gun and sent a heavy charge of buckshot into the creature's belly about where it emerged from the water.

"A visible tremor passed through his body; his head fell down, bringing Jack down with frightful velocity. The poor fellow was hurled against the side of the boat with a force, as I thought, that would kill him instantly, and landing the ax he had in his hand far out on dry land.

"It was now apparent that my shot had not only wounded the monster but had angered him to a rather dangerous and alarming degree. Instantly his head was again on high, deafening hisses came from his throat, and the waters for a hundred feet seaward were churned into foam by the horrid writhing of his body.

"Again I raised my gun and discharged the other barrel. If my first shot had angered him, my second shot worked him into a frenzy that knew no bounds.

"Throwing back his great hooded head in true serpentine style, he began to strike at our boat. At one time fastening his jaws upon our starboard gunwale, he quickly wrenched off a piece of solid timber five feet long and two inches thick, as easily, apparently, as a man would a piece of paper. Throwing his body into a series of great vertical coils eight feet in diameter, he completely encircled the boat, and with one constriction crushed it into a shapeless mass.

"After crushing the boat the monster did not immediately uncoil himself, but lay some minutes with fragments still in his embrace, while his ever-restless tail whipped the surface of the sea. In one of its gyrations the end of the tail fell upon the beach and, with what must have been superhuman agility, I seized the ax that had been hurled from Jack's clutch, and with one blow cut off ten or fifteen feet of the wriggling end. I was esteeming this a most valuable prize, but before I could secure it the slimy mass wriggled into the water and was lost.

"From this time the great monster evidently began to weaken from loss of blood, which was pouring in streams from his head and the wound given him by the ax. Slowly regaining his normal position in the water, the creature withdrew toward the open sea and was soon out of sight.

"When I first saw him swimming squarely abreast of me, I should judge from the elevated head to where the sea was lashed by the end of his tail the distance was 200 feet. The great flattened head was hooded like that of an East Indian cobra, and from the tip of the nose to the insertion of the neck would have measured five feet. The head was fully three feet wide, but appeared to be deficient in vertical depth. The eyes were set just forward of the hooded appendage and were as large as the eyes of an ox. There were no indications of a dorsal fin or rudimental feet, as have been attributed by some former observers to the so called sea monsters. But Jack claimed he had very large horns.

"After several hours of work and administering several doses of medicine, Jack was brought around all right. From the nature of the wounds inflicted upon Jack it was apparent the monster was not venomous."

Another encounter with an Alaska sea monster was reported by the Stroller's Weekly *on August 8, 1928. The headline read: "Sea Serpent Killed in Chatham Straits." The principles in this story, Commissioner Sprague and Captain Smith, were well known in the territory of Alaska. Additionally, they were experienced seamen and not likely to have mistaken some known sea animal for the creature they saw.*

Death of a Sea Serpent

The Territorial Fish Commissioner, A. J. Sprague, was a witness to the following sighting:

Sprague was out on official business on the *Yakobi*, accompanied by the owner of the latter, Captain Tom Smith. They were near Morris Reef, which is at the junction of Chatham and Pearl Straits, when there appeared before their eyes at a distance not to exceed 100 yards a monster of the deep that was fully 300 feet in length, about four feet in diameter, of a greenish blue color, and which glided side-to-side in swimming very much like a snake.

As the animal, serpent, or whatever it was swam rather slowly, Sprague and Smith had a splendid view of it. The former seized a rifle and, as the body of the thing would appear above the crest of the waves, fired a number of shots at it. He is confident that one or more of the leaden pellets reached vital parts as it seemed to writhe in the water and finally reared its long snake-like head several feet above the water and then disappeared into the depths.

The *Yakobi* remained in the vicinity for some time in the hope that the huge body would come again to the surface, in which event, in case life was extinct, it was the intention of the two men to throw a hook into it and tow it to some point where it could be beached and examined. Judging from the thickness of the thing, it was estimated that every four feet would weigh a ton, which would give it a total weight of seventy-five tons.

The locality in which the monster was seen was later visited but nothing was seen of it. Mr. Sprague is certain it was unable to digest the bullets by which it was hit and its dead body now reposes with other mysteries of the deep.

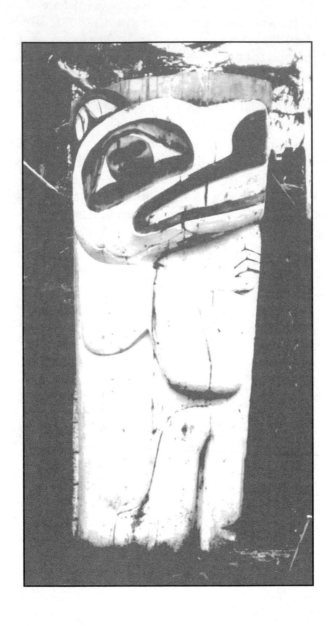

Strange Inhabitants

As pioneers penetrated the wildernesses of Alaska and the Yukon, they encountered strange new tribes of people. Modern anthropologists have identified most of the tribes described by the early pioneers, but a few have never been sighted again and remain unknown to this day. The possible existence of such tribes — including black Natives, blond Natives with blue eyes, and cannibals — remains a mystery.

Often early-day prospectors heard stories about strange tribes from the Native people they knew. The Dawson Indians, for example, have a legend of intermarrying with a white race long before miners and trappers came to the Klondike. In the Copper River country, Athabaskan elders related stories of "monkey people" who lived in caves.

Equally inexplicable were the feats of the occult performed by Native shamans, or "medicine men." According to turn-of-the-century reports, some of these men could perform acts that defied all known natural laws.

According to legend, the most powerful of the Tlingit shamans was Koo-Nok-Aa-Tee, a hermit who lived on an island near Sitka. In 1889, Captain J. E. Rowe and Dr. H. R. Corson, along with Tlingit guides, visited the grave of the shaman. The Tlingits exhibited great awe and respect for the Koo-Nok-Aa-Tee ("powerful human being"). Dr. Corson tried to gain more information on the medicine man, but the Tlingits were reluctant to discuss him any further. A reporter for the (Sitka) Alaskan *interviewed Rowe and Corson, and the following story appeared in the* Alaskan *on October 12, 1889.*

The Storm Master

The Storm Master's tribe was unknown, but he may have been a Kwakiutl, as he was cannibalistic. The shaman lived in a small hut on an island in Sitka Sound. His hut was surrounded by human bones carved into strange figures, and rattles and charms to attract his Helper Spirits.

Near his hut was a point of land that jutted out into the sea. At the end of this point was a large, jagged rock. When winter storms raged, the shaman would climb to the top of this rock and gaze into the storm, absorbing the power of the elements.

A party of Indians on their way to Sitka in large seagoing canoes were the first to report the shaman's power.

At the day of his appearance a savage winter storm raged. The sky was black, the rain poured down in torrents. Great waves dashed against the rocks and cliffs, making a deafening and roaring noise, striking fear into the hearts of the travelers. As the storm swept the canoes toward a rocky promontory to certain destruction, the Indians saw a man standing on a point. Unaffected by the wild winds or rain, he stood motionlessly upon that great rock, gazing upward with eyes fixed on the heavens. Raising his arms to the storm, the winds and waves abated. The canoes were transported to the beach by an unseen power.

From that time on, if the Indians were about to make a trip in their canoes, they would come to the medicine man and beg him to insure good weather.

The Indians believed he could control the storms and cause them to divert from their course or to subside according to his will. For many years, the shaman lived on his island and was known from Puget Sound to Yakutat Bay for his power over the weather.

Koo-Nok-Aa-Tee died on the rocky promontory during a storm in the 1860s. A party of Indians found him lying on the great rock, his face toward the sky, his arms outstretched. The Indians buried the medicine man near a cluster of cedar trees.

But the story did not end at his death.

The rock upon which the shaman displayed his mysterious powers went through an amazing transformation. During his life, this rock was unusually rugged, so much so that it was difficult to climb. But at his death, the nature of the stone changed completely. The rock, instead of being rugged as it was before his death, was changed into a flat, level, tabled surface large enough for a house.

Even today the Indians guard and protect the grave of the Storm Master, the most powerful of all the medicine men.

The following account was based on the experiences of E. A. Von Hasslocher, a trader at Tuxekan. He was an interesting character in his own right, as he held the rank of Tlingit chief. How he became a chief is an unusual story. When the trader helped federal authorities capture two Tlingits who had murdered a white man, the Tlingits' friends swore to kill Von Hasslocher. The head chief of the Raven Clan adopted the merchant, making him a chief. Under Tlingit law, anyone who killed a chief was to make restitution of hundreds of blankets, canoes, containers of oil, and other items. These payments were so burdensome as to impoverish the killer and bring shame to his clan. Consequently, the plot against Von Hasslocher was abandoned.

Because of his rank as Tlingit chief, Von Hasslocher was allowed to participate in the sacred fire ceremony, probably the only white man ever afforded that honor. His story was written by E. S. Harrison and appeared in the December 1909 issue of the Alaska-Yukon Magazine.

Mystic Fire-Eater

In 1891, a great potlatch was given by the Tlingits of Tuxekan, and the Hydah Indians had been invited. Quantities of food had been prepared for the visitors. There was dried fish and fresh fish, seal oil and candlefish oil, edible seaweed in great quantities, and the game of Prince of Wales Island. From the trader's store had been secured barrels of sugar, bolts of calico, boxes of hardtack, and many pieces of tin and glassware, utensils, and trinkets, for this was to be a big potlatch.

The appointed time arrived, but the guests did not. After a long wait, Ska Owa, the shaman, was called upon to make medicine and bring the guests or tell the reason why they did not come.

Ska Owa was very old. He claimed to have lived more than a hundred years. Although gray and slightly stooping, he possessed unusual vigor for an old man. He was tall and thin, with regular features, an intellectual forehead, and great luminous eyes that shone with supernatural luster when he was making medicine.

The ceremonies were under way when a messenger arrived at the house of Von Hasslocher and told him that the medicine man wanted him at the ceremony. Hastily obeying the summons, he found a dozen or more chiefs of different ranks squatted around the fire that was burning on the gravel floor of the medicine house. The fire was made of resinous logs, and it burned with a fierce flame. Each chief held in his hand a stick with which he beat a weird tattoo to a chant, while the old medicine man, standing erect among them in the regalia of his office, worked himself into a frenzy of the highest nerve tension. It was explained to Mr. Von Hasslocher that after the medicine man purified himself by fire, the shaman's spirit would leave his body and visit the village of the Hydahs.

Seated in the circle with his Raven Clan, the white chief beat time with his medicine stick. Soon after his arrival an Indian squatted beside him and said to him in the Tlingit tongue: "The medicine man will ask you for fire. When he asks, give him a coal."

The white chief picked up another stick,

intending to offer the coal by the aid of these two sticks, but his neighbor said to him: "No! You must take up the fire with your hand; the medicine man will not receive it in any other way."

Presently the medicine man stopped his incantation and asked the white chief for fire. Mr. Von Hasslocher raked out a glowing coal the size of an English walnut. Picking it up he laid it on the palm of his left hand, as he was instructed to do by the Native squatting beside him. He arose and presented it to the medicine man. Of course he was in a hurry to get rid of it, but the medicine man was very deliberate in his actions. He took the coal and placed it in his mouth, chewed it into fragments, and spat it out. Again he called for fire and this time the white chief gave him a larger coal. It lighted up the cavity of the shaman's mouth and glowed through the thin tissue of his cheeks. Three times the white chief gave him fire, each time holding the coal, which under ordinary conditions would inflict a severe burn, but the hand was not even scorched. Every chief in the building fed the old man with fire, and when the ceremony was ended, he was unharmed. The shaman then went into a trance. When he awoke, he said his spirit had visited the Hydah village, and that they would arrive in two days.

The next day the shaman sent for the white chief and examined the hand that held the live coal. The old man's eyes lighted up as he grunted his satisfaction over the absence of any trace of a burn. The medicine had enabled the white man to perform his part of the ceremony successfully.

The following day the Hydahs arrived, and the potlatch was the most successful ever held by the Tlingits.

Early Alaska and Yukon newspapers often featured articles on the discovery of unknown tribes by prospectors and trappers as they pushed into the wilderness. Most of these tribes can now be identified as belonging to various Indian and Eskimo groups, but some are still unknown. The Stroller's Weekly *for September 13, 1930, carried the following story about a tribe of northern pygmies.*

Pygmies of the North Pole

In June of 1911, John Weizl was with a party of scientists headed by Captain Yvolnoff, a Russian explorer. At a location about 730 miles northwest of the North Pole, the Eskimo guides found tracks of very small size which they pronounced as human. They followed the tracks, finally losing them in the snow. The dogs picked up the trail a short distance further on and followed them until they ended at a small hole dug in the snow. The hole was too small for any of the party to enter, but they finally sent in one of the dogs. The dog soon came out, seeming not to like what he had discovered. The party waited for a time and finally one of the occupants stepped outside. He appeared frightened, but was soon calmed. No one could understand him. The Eskimos had never seen such people.

Finally the little man called others out of the holes in the snow cave and it was discovered there were four families of twenty-seven people. They were clad in very fine skins. Apparently they had no fires

41

or weapons — nothing but themselves and their skin clothing. There was open water in the vicinity and the Natives lived on small fish, somewhat like trout, which were present in immense quantities. The pygmies scooped the fish out with their bare hands and ate them on the spot, raw. They ate only the backs and threw the rest away.

Not having any photographic apparatus with the party, Mr. Weizl made a drawing of the little man. He was about three and one-half feet tall, very thin and weighing about thirty-five or forty pounds. The head was almost triangular-shaped, coming to a peak, with a small tuft of hair at the top. The ears were enormous. Their voices were high and shrill and totally unlike the Eskimos.

Captain Yvolnoff expressed a determination to form another expedition to the locality, but he died in 1913. Another expedition was planned after Capt. Yvolnoff's death, but was stopped by the World War. Mr. Weizl has the exact location of the party in his possession and says he hopes to again visit the locality.

The following story was recounted by Reverend Arthur R. Wright, a missionary in Alaska in the early 1900s. Reverend Wright was half Athabaskan, the son of a white man and an Indian mother. Educated by the church, he treated the stories of his people as myths and legends. Yet Athabaskan elders tell the story of the Tail Men as a matter of history. Reverend Wright's story was originally published in the Cordova Daily News *on February 7, 1924.*

The Tail Men

On a recent trip over to the Copper River the Indians drew my attention to numerous holes in an embankment we passed. On inquiring of them I was told that those were the holes of "men with tails." With some questioning, this is the tale I heard.

In the Selina River country were rolling hills on which numerous caribou roamed. The Indians who subsisted on meat were lured to this district by the abundance of game. And years ago at the mouth of the Selina River they built a large Indian village.

One day a dog brought into the camp the tail of a fish. No one had caught any fish, and it puzzled the Indians as to how the animal got the fish. Finally it was decided to search the district to determine if there were any other tribes in the area.

A group went out to search for the unknown people. When several of the searchers did not return, the tribe knew something was wrong.

What had happened to these men?

Finally one of their most skillful trackers was sent in search of the missing scouts.

He made his way cautiously through the country. At length he came upon a hidden trail through the woods. Across the path at intervals was stretched a rope made of grass. This he examined very carefully.

"A trap . . . an alarm," he thought.

He continued to follow the trail, which led to a group of caves he could see in the distance.

Very cautiously he strained eye and ear for sight or sound of anything unusual. Finally from out of the numerous caves came men with tails. They had all the appearance of normal men except for a tail, which dragged behind them. He was much surprised to see them use these tails as their chief means of locomotion. They curled their tails forward between their legs and recoiled in such a manner as to push themselves forward.

As the scout watched them, keeping to windward to avoid being detected by scent, they kicked what looked to him like a ball. On observing it more closely, the Indian recognized to his horror the head of one of his companions.

He watched them rush to and fro, capering about with much shouting and hideous glee, evidently having a game of ball with the head.

He quickly noted their number, also the number of caves, and returned back to his camp.

After he made his report, a group of men and boys gathered, and an attack was planned on the village of Tail Men. They decided to seal off the caves with fire and smoke, thus killing the people inside.

It was raining when they reached the caves and the Tail Men were all inside. Each group was detailed to a cave. With burning brands and brush, the Indians rushed the caves and plugged the openings.

As the attackers stood guard, through the fire came flights of arrows. Soon this stopped. After all signs of life from the Tail Men had ceased, the Indians returned homeward.

The Tail Men were no more a menace to the Indians. Today all that remains of them are this legend, their caves, and numerous arrowheads.

Thus ended the story, and someday I hope to return and try to find out more about these Tail Men.

If Reverend Wright ever returned to the caves to search for the remains of the Tail Men, he did not make his findings public.

Places of Mystery

During the exploration of Alaska and northwestern Canada, prospectors and trappers recounted tales of discovering amazing places in the primeval wilderness. There were vast mountain ranges whose peaks reached to the sky . . . glacial lakes and wide, slow-moving rivers . . . arctic plains inhabited by great herds of caribou . . . and above it all, the northern lights sweeping across the night sky.

Today the majestic beauty of the Northland is known around the world. And yet some of the places described by early adventurers have never been rediscovered. Many told stories of lush tropical valleys, teeming with fish and game, hidden in vast mountain ranges. Others reported seeing detailed visions of ancient walled cities. One prospector claimed to have found a whole forest full of petrified trees as hard as stone.

Skeptics say these stories were the products of imagination and exaggeration, but perhaps we will someday rediscover these places of wonder. Vast areas of Alaska and Canada are still unknown wilderness.

One of the most persistent stories of the North Country told of a lost tropical valley located in the arctic or sub-arctic wilderness. According to prospectors and trappers, these valleys were paradises, heated by subterranean volcanic activity which produced lush plant growth and stands of timber. Herds of fat mountain sheep, caribou, and moose grazed in the meadows, unafraid of man. The warm lakes were filled with flocks of ducks and geese.

For the most part, these tales were based on Native legends. But an account of a hidden paradise by mining engineer Frank Perry was fairly specific as to location, and was corroborated by other prospectors and trappers. His story was published in the Alaska Weekly on June 26, 1925.

The Valley of Eden

For seventeen years, with only two pack dogs to carry his equipment, Frank Perry explored the unknown subarctic regions until, by chance, he came upon a vast paradise in the midst of snow-covered mountains.

Crossing a range one winter and reaching the crest, Perry prepared to descend into the next valley when he was surprised to find the area covered with heavy fog. This valley was approximately 200 miles long and about forty wide. Rivers of hot water ran through it, fed by hundreds of hot springs. These springs bubbled out of the ground, condensed, and formed a layer of fog.

Perry remained in the valley and its neighborhood for a year. Never before in his experiences had he seen so many wild animals which congregated there for the luxuriant vegetation made possible by the heat generated by the springs. In the valley were hundreds of mountain sheep, goats, caribou, and moose, with bears and other fur-bearing animals.

Due to the exceptionally good grazing in the valley, Perry stated that the moose and caribou looked like the pictures of the old Norman horse — almost square from fat — and they were so tame that he walked among them and could almost touch them as they fed.

This country was never visited by the Indians because of imprints of huge three-toed prehistoric animals found in the sandstones and shales. Indians thought these monsters still roamed the country and, although they knew it to be a hunter's paradise, they gave the valley a wide berth.

In addition to the hot springs, there were mineral springs of various descriptions.

The black soil was of a depth which Perry estimated at between sixty seven and seventy feet, on a clay subsoil. The trees' growth was abnormal, some being two to three feet in diameter. The ordinary wild rosebushes had stems as thick as a man's forearm, and so dense Perry found it impossible to force a way through them. The willows grew to tree size, and it was possible to walk along the branches. Some of the trunks were fully one and a half foot through. Vines grew to a length of about sixty feet, and nettles and ferns were higher than a man's head.

During the winter there was no frost in this valley. For twenty-five miles there was open land suitable for ranching, the width of the valley being estimated at four miles. In other sections it was a mixed, park-like country which would need clearing of birch and willow, but there were considerable areas open in patches. Perry stated that in addition to the marvels of vegetation, the minerals were quite equal in their unusual quantities. Rich formations of gold, silver, and copper were found. He struck three veins which were particularly good; those were about forty feet wide and 150 feet long. But there were thousands of others, said Perry. Coal there was, too — a mountain full — with iron in proximity. One coal seam measured 800 feet across the strike. The largest iron ore seam ran about two hundred feet thick, as far as the explorer could judge. In addition, oil formations were found, with numerous seepages. The ore samples Perry displayed at Edmonton were very rich, and appeared to substantiate his claims.

Though to some the whole story may sound like a fairy tale, Perry stated that his discovery was real, and he planned to take a party in to investigate and confirm what is written here. According to Perry's description, the valley lies between the coastal range and Liard and Fort Nelson Rivers in the Cassiar Mountains.

Frank Perry's claims of having discovered a tropical valley were supported by the testimony of Captain Sam C. Scotte, who said he had lived for two years in the paradise described by Perry. Scotte's account appeared in the Alaska Weekly *on July 25, 1924.*

Winter in Paradise

Captain Sam C. Scotte has a cabin in the valley described by Frank Perry and spent two winters there. He expects to depart for that tropical paradise in the near future.

It is reached via the Stikine River and Telegraph Creek, being in the Cassiar Range of mountains. The valley is about twenty miles in length and from three to four miles in width.

There is a fair-sized stream running through the valley. The valley is swampy, with many small lakes and timbered flats. The soil is a rich black loam, adapted to truck gardening. Captain Scotte says he raised all the garden truck he needed for his table.

Warm springs are abundant and are responsible for the tropical nature of the region. These springs, however, are not in the valley proper, but are in the rim of the foothills. A strange characteristic is that the water from the springs is ice cold in the summer and warm during the winter. There is a heavy rainfall during the summer, and thunder and lightning frequently occur.

Captain Scotte bears out the statement of Frank

Perry, whom he knows and who is alleged to have discovered this strange land some years ago, as to the strange animals that inhabit this land. Scotte himself says he saw white deer there, a species that he never saw or heard of before, and that Casca John, an old Indian, told him about animals very similar to musk oxen that inhabited the region.

The tropical valley is a veritable bird land, says Scotte. During the summer months, there is one continuous song in the air.

That the valley is tropical is perhaps due to the fact that it is 3,000 feet lower than the general contour of the country surrounding.

Another witness to the existence of the tropical valley was Colonel J. Scott Williams from Montreal. While exploring British Columbia and the Yukon by airplane for three months, Williams claimed to have spent a half-day in the beautiful, secret valley somewhere in the Liard River country. His account was published on September 24, 1925, in the Wrangell Sentinel.

Where the Waters Run Warm

A visit to the mysterious valley far beyond the path of the white man in the North Country, beyond the Liard Trading Post, was described here Monday by Col. J. Scott Williams of Montreal, who arrived here after completing the first prospecting trip ever conducted in British Columbia by airplane.

The description of the valley as a subtropical one is correct, according to Colonel Williams. It contains numerous hot springs, grass, and verdure of amazing growth due, it is thought, to the warmth generated by the springs. The soil is very fertile, and of a quality quite unrivaled. The flowers, which include violets, are unequaled for size, while berries and currants are amazing for their productiveness.

"For nearly three months, we lived chiefly on moose meat, mountain sheep steaks, and other wild game with beans," said Colonel Williams. "It was a fine chance to get into the tropical valley and have a good feed of potatoes, grown there from seed that wintered in the ground. There were also onions growing there that were planted by a prospector named Smith who was there the previous year. They were all large and of excellent quality. The raspberries were the largest I have ever seen.

"The valley is certainly a wonderful place, and it abounds with wild game. We were only there half a day, as we were not out on a pleasure trip, but we had time to bathe in the warm water and relax after our strenuous work seeking gold."

Col. Williams said that among the other interesting things he saw in the North were a white moose, doubtless an albino, and also white bear similar to the Beacon Hill Park animal in Victoria.

Speaking of the country generally, Col. Williams said there were immense tracks of well-wooded land that looked as if it would be easy to cultivate and could be used for agriculture, but it is all so far from human habitation that it will not be used for many a day, he thinks.

*Hank Russell and his partner, Jack Lee, were sea otter
hunters, trappers, and prospectors. Their account of a tropical valley was not as well documented as that of Frank
Perry, but then most prospectors were protective of their
discoveries and therefore reluctant to discuss them in any
detail. Russell and Lee planned to return to their valley
and spend the winter hunting and trapping. The* Valdez
Miner *for November 11, 1922, carried their story.*

An Oasis in the Arctic

Hank Russell and Jack Lee climbed a high arctic mountain pass one morning, and discovered a
green valley in the midst of snow-covered peaks.
Determined to investigate, they traveled for hours
over the steep range, hunting for a way to descend
into the area. Finally they found a narrow canyon
that came out into a valley several miles broad. They
stated that the valley apparently had been the bed
of an ancient volcano.

Entering the valley the first thing they noticed
was the warmth. Parkas and furs were speedily laid
aside.

Looking over the valley, the prospectors could
see shoulder-high green grass, with many vari-hued
flowers on the slopes of the towering hills. Stands
of timber three feet in diameter grew throughout
the valley. Birds by the thousands were seen, prin-
cipally warblers, with a few robins. On a small lake

about a mile long and a half-mile across were flocks of geese and ducks.

Broad game trails were worn in the soil, and great herds of caribou and other animals gazed curiously at the invaders. Numerous brown and black bears were seen at the edge of the valley, near where the snow line came down from the high hills.

Mr. Russell declared that while they remained in the valley their meals were cooked over a fumarole. The ground was so warm they discarded their sleeping bags and slept on piles of grass.

In looking over the valley, the prospectors found tracks of several animals of species unknown to them. These tracks were too large for bears, being some eighteen inches in diameter and perfectly round with three depressions in the front of the track resembling toes.

Had they been living in a prehistoric age, the prospectors would have sworn the tracks to be those of mastodon or mammoth. A close search of the valley revealed no animal large enough to make tracks anywhere near this size, and unless the creature lived in the warm waters of the lake, they were unable to account for its whereabouts.

They also saw bear tracks of enormous size, and in places the bushes were torn up for several yards, branches being broken many feet from the ground.

Mr. Russell believed that the tropical paradise was caused by volcanic fires existing close to the surface of the earth. He stated that the earth was uncomfortably warm to their moccasins, and in many spots steam jets spouted many feet into the air, causing a dense fog in their vicinity.

The walls around the old crater were about 1,500

feet in height and very precipitous, the only entrance being along the banks of the river through the canyon.

Hank Russell and Jack Lee never revealed any additional details to the Miner *about their hidden paradise. Nothing more is known, either, about Frank Perry and Sam Scotte, or the tropical valley they discovered. Apparently these men took the location of these secret places with them to the grave.*

In the arid regions of the world, mirages are a common optical phenomenon produced by rays of light hitting a layer of heated air. But in Alaska and the Yukon these atmospheric conditions rarely, if ever, occur. Yet early travelers to the Northland reported seeing visions of fantastically detailed images. In the July 25, 1924, issue of the Alaska Weekly, *C. L. Thompson described a mirage he saw on his way to the gold fields in 1898.*

Miraculous Mirage

Our steamer sailed from Seattle on May 30, 1898. It took us thirty days from Seattle to St. Michael. Ordinarily this voyage can be made in from seven to ten days. Our steamer had in tow the barge *Admiral* and the river steamer *Lovering*, reducing our speed to four knots per hour.

We followed the coastline as closely as safety would permit, which gave us an opportunity to put into a sheltered port in case of an approaching storm.

It was about noon on our fifteenth day out, when our boat drew near Kodiak Island. There was a perfect calm, the ocean a perfect mirror. Here we saw the most wonderful mirage ever witnessed by man.

There came to view, from the water level, the formation of a big city, with all the streets, big buildings, churches, and the usual street traffic. There were wharves, and riverboats plying on the water, and boats lying at the docks loading and unloading. At the same time, an elevated railroad trestle came to the water's edge and a mammoth buttress arose to meet the trestle, and while this was being done, across the river, about a thousand feet to the left, a palisade of rocks, forming the riverbank, with a canyon and wooded dell, was a huge buttress starting from the water to correspond with the one on the city side.

Then simultaneously from the buttresses came the construction of the steel cantilever, with the bottom and top cords of the mammoth bridge that was to span the river.

The cords and steel trusses showed every brace as they gradually approached until they met in the center of the 1,000-foot span, which was about fifty feet deep at the junction.

Under this span we plainly saw the ships. I mention this to show that the arch was clean-cut, with no backgrounds. On top of the cap cord of the span were the ties and rails, forming the railroad track, with clear space between rail and top cord. When this was completed, out from the city came an engine, tender, and three passenger coaches — the type used those days, with open, not closed, vestibules as used now, and showing brakes, wheels, draw bars, and coupling pins, every truss red and tool boxes under the floors of the cars, all in place. This train passed over the bridge at the rate of five or six miles an hour. You could see through the windows and see one ship in the lead.

The greatest surprise of all, and one that caused much comment among the boys, was the sight of the engineer leaning out of the cab and pulling the bell cord, with the bell swinging in unison with the motion. Everything about the engine was complete. Even the bell cord was visible with the glasses. I watched it every minute.

When the rear of the train had reached three-fourths of the way across the span, the span was cut as if with a saw and each side was telescoped into itself. Then everything vanished as if by magic. Where we had seen the city was now the island of Kodiak, not a half-mile distant.

I turned to Captain Patterson and said, "What do you think of that?"

His reply was, "I don't think a picture like that was ever seen by mortal man before; it is wonderful. In all my experience as a sea captain for thirty years, I have never seen anything like it before."

The mirage, as seen at the time, was in perfectly clear blue sky and a clean-cut photograph could not have been more striking. I pronounced it once as a reproduction of the cantilever bridge at St. Louis, as it was the largest cantilever bridge in the world at that time. It amazed me that a mirage with such perfect clarity could be reflected some 3,000 miles away!

I have been asked how long this mirage was in sight, and I would estimate about five minutes' duration. Five more members of my party came on deck and saw the last half of the phenomenon.

I have seen many mirages on the plains during the 1860s and 1870s when I hunted buffalo. But none of them was as awe-inspiring as that mirage near Kodiak in June of 1898.

One of the most famous mirages, the "Silent City," was branded a hoax because pioneer Juneau miner Dick Willoughby faked a picture of the mirage and sold copies to tourists. He was doing well until someone recognized the image of the "Silent City" as a photo of Manchester, England, taken by a professional photographer.

However, several people still claimed to have seen the real "Silent City." George T. Hall, a mining engineer, was one. In an interview with the Seattle Post Intelligencer *in February of 1901, he reaffirmed his sighting of the mirage. His comments were in response to a statement by W. M. Brooks, a prospector who argued that the mirage was only a figment of Dick Willoughby's imagination.*

Hall's statement was reprinted in the Daily Alaskan *on February 12, 1901.*

The Silent City

I do not care to enter in a controversy with Mr. Brooks regarding his claim, but he never saw the "Silent City of Alaska." It has, however, been seen by scores of intelligent people in Alaska, and by a number of noted travelers, among them Captain A. C. Hanson of Dawson; Albert Cody, United States Inspector for the Yukon; Colonel J. C. Bowie; and J. N. Ransmiller, a well-known mining man of Washington and Alaska.

In 1889 Mrs. C. S. Longstreet, a well-known writer and traveler, visited Alaska and spent four weeks in the vicinity of Muir Glacier. She saw the mirage, which resembled an ancient city.

On January 17, 1899, I was with a party crossing Lake Laberge. . . . Suddenly something loomed up ahead of us, and there we saw rising from the mountains a misty picture of an ancient city. Each object was perfectly outlined. The sight was too vivid to doubt its reality.

The city appeared to be situated on some large body of water, and we could plainly see individual blocks of stone in the seawall, and the waves beating against it. The sun was just going down at the time and the windows of the phantom city seemed to flame with light.

I cannot tell whether the mirage we saw is the same which has been seen from Mount Fairweather or Muir Glacier, but it resembles descriptions which I have heard of those other mirages. It appeared like an ancient walled city. The others in our party will verify this story.

Percy Snider, the author of the following account, does not identify the location of Coal Creek or the site of the petrified forest he discovered nearby. However, near Wood-chopper on the Yukon River, there is a Coal Creek and a group of hills called the White Mountains, so this area fits Snider's description of the place where he made his strange discovery. This story appeared in the Daily Klondike Nugget *on March 30, 1901.*

A Petrified Forest

"While on a prospecting trip in the Rockies in the summer of 1898, I made what I consider to be a very remarkable discovery," said Mr. Percy Snider, a well-known sourdough.

"There were three of us in the party, William Holden, William Blackburn, and myself.

"We were investigating some coal property on Coal Creek and thought before we came to Dawson, we would make a trip into the mountains, which were only a few miles' distance from where our camp was located. At that time, I was just recovering from an attack of scurvy and was not very strong. Our food had been stolen a short time before, and we were compelled to live on what game we could kill.

"We started in the morning and reached the foot-hills of the mountains about noon, when my legs suddenly gave out, and I sat down to rest. The rest of the party, thinking I had played out, left me there to rest while they went in search of game, expecting to return to me in the evening. After they had been gone and I had been sitting there for a short time, my weakness suddenly left, and I arose feeling stronger than at any time since my sickness.

"I followed my companions for a way, but found they had too much of a start and that it would be impossible for me to overtake them, so I started to cut across, thinking I might intercept them. My path led me to the foot of the mountains, which I succeeded in scaling by taking a very circuitous route. It was on the top of this peak where I made what I consider a very remarkable discovery.

"There is a plateau on top of the mountain which will contain from ten to twenty acres. This is several hundred feet above timberline, but on this plateau there were thirty to forty trees, just about the size of the trees on the Klondike, but entirely bereft of branches and with a surface as smooth and polished as if they had been just put through a polishing process.

"A careful examination of the ground failed to reveal any sign of fallen branches or limbs, and the only growing thing to be seen in the whole area was a short moss. Upon close examination of the trees, I found them to be as hard as ivory, and I could make no impression on them with my knife or a rock. I tried to shake them but found them immovable.

"The only conclusion I could come to was that they are relics of olden times when this was a tropical country and that particular peak may have been an island.

"I stayed there that night, and the next morning I made my way back to the place I had left and found my companions just organizing a searching party to go look for me."

"My story will probably be looked upon as sort of fishy," said Mr. Snider in conclusion, "but I am firmly convinced in my own mind that those trees are petrified and I intend to make a trip there this summer and use dynamite, if necessary, to get some specimens from them."

Messengers from Beyond

Among the most baffling stories that have come out of the gold rush country are those that tell of encounters with shades and spirits.

The earliest recorded ghost story in Alaska is the classic tale of the "Blue Lady," the ghostly princess of Baranof's Castle (see photo, left). The princess died in the 1840s and presumably haunted the castle from that date until the building burned in 1894.

In recent times, the nearby Bishop's House reportedly has been visited by an apparition wearing a Russian-style dress. To this day, the gold rush town of Skagway is said to harbor several ghosts, the most famous being the ghostly bride who haunts the Golden North Hotel.

Other stories tell of helpful spirits that have led lost ships to safety, assisted miners in making their fortunes, and offered warnings to those in peril. Perhaps, although the days of the gold rush are long gone, the spirits of some of its pioneers have remained behind to watch over the North Country.

Baranof's Castle was built to house Alaska's first governor, Alexander Baranof. Toward the end of its days, the castle was a gloomy, desolate building perched upon a hill overlooking Sitka Harbor. It was believed to be haunted by a beautiful young woman dressed in a pale blue gown. The "princess," according to tradition, was a young woman of noble birth who fell in love with a young Russian naval officer. When forced by her father to marry another man, she committed suicide on her wedding night. Her spirit was said to appear in the drawing room, where she had been found dead, or in the cupola gazing out to sea, where she could wait for her lover's ship to return.

The following account was written by John Arctanger in 1911 and is taken from his book, The Lady in Blue.

The Ghostly Princess of Baranof's Castle

How long I slept I do not know, but the first sensation of which I was aware was of someone tapping me lightly on the shoulder. I raised myself quickly on the elbow, and there: — was it a vision, or what was it?

By the side of my bed, not farther away than I could have touched her with my outstretched hand, stood a beautiful woman. She was dressed in a pale blue silk dress with a satin sash of the same color, tied around a tapering narrow waist and falling in great lengths down over the unnaturally large hips, almost to the bottom of the wide crinoline skirt.

The extremely décolleté corsage exhibited a lovely

neck and snowy, finely chiseled shoulders, while the arms were covered with very full bishop sleeves, with narrow bands at the wrists.

On her black hair, so black that it seemed almost blue, which hung down in corkscrew curls on both sides of a most beautiful face, was resting a silver band in the shape of a tiara or crown. Her black eyes were so large and piercing that they seemed almost like two burning coals, but as she closed them for a moment, as with a painful movement, there came over the face an expression of despair, sorrow, and suffering so intense, as I have never seen depicted on a human face. . . .

In her left hand the lady in blue held a silver candlestick, in which was a burning wax candle. With the right she made several quick, imperious motions, as if pointing over her shoulder to the door of the room.

She then turned. And with her right hand around the flame of the candle, as if sheltering it from the draft, the magnificent Juno-like form slowly glided over the polished floor to the door, which opened as in obedience to her silent command and half closed again behind her.

Although it seemed impossible for me to make the slightest move while she was standing near my bed, now that she had disappeared behind the door I felt an irresistible impulse take possession of me to follow her out in the hall, and, if possible, fathom the mystery.

I jumped out of bed and ran to the door as quickly as I could, for fear that she would disappear without my knowing whither.

Reaching the door I was surprised to find it closed, but it readily responded to my eager grasp, and letting my eyes flash first in one direction and then in another, I felt my heart beat faster upon discovering the lady in blue gliding silently along the corridor in the direction of the great salon, from which were wafted toward the place where I stood the measures of a stately minuet. She was still shading the flame of the candle with her hand.

Then suddenly I lost sight of her and of the candle, which had been fluttering like a distant star in the dark hallway.

I hastened my steps and was soon rewarded. Only a short distance, and an open door showed a staircase leading upward. From six or seven steps up her candle threw just enough light to show the stairs.

I ran up the steps, determined that she should not escape me.

As I reached the landing, I observed her by the window on the opposite side of a large glass cupola, peering out into the dark night, shading her eyes with her beautiful and transparent hand.

Oh, the sadness and sorrow in that face!

I was about to speak, to comfort her . . . when I heard coming from down below, from out of the darkness of the night, in the deep basso tones of the Russian sentry stationed on the bastion in front of the castle, these words: "One o'clock and all is well."

As if these words of human voice had awakened the lady in blue from out of a trance, I observed a sudden tremor in the hand shading her eyes.

An awful, unearthly cry of anguish resounded in my ears.

The candlestick fell to the floor with a crash and all was — darkness.

Determined to do what I could to assist the sad-eyed, sorrowing lady, I crept cautiously across the tiles over to the place where I had seen her stand but a moment before, and groped around in the dark. My hands touched the panes of the window against which she had leaned, but she had vanished with the flickering flame. . . .

I was satisfied that the apparition, whether human or spirit, had gone out of my conscious existence. . . .

I was not so sure, as I was an hour ago, that there were no ghosts.

The lady in blue seemed too real, too flesh-and-blood-like, too human to be a spirit, but still no human being could have disappeared in the twinkling of an eye as she did, just as if she had sunk through the floor.

Critics of the Baranof's Castle ghost story argue that it was fabricated to keep people out of the deserted building. They ignore the experience of the Corporal of the Guard who was on duty at the castle in November of 1888. He gave a chilling, unadorned report of a supernatural encounter in the deserted castle. His account appeared in the (Sitka) Alaskan on November 10, 1888.

Phantom Footsteps

To the Editor of the *Alaskan.*

Sir, — During the time that the castle was being prepared for the ball recently given by the officers of the USS *Pinta*, a large number of valuable flags for decorating the walls were left in the castle over several nights. To prevent any light-fingered individual from disturbing these flags, the Corporal of the Guard visited the building every night, hourly.

I do not believe in ghosts, but when, during my tour of night duty, I visited the rooms of the castle I could not help feeling a peculiar sensation pass over me. The oppressive silence which prevails there in the dead hour of a still night is awful. A visit which I made at one o'clock in the morning I shall never forget. It is impressed upon my mind so forcibly because it is connected with something I cannot account for. I had a lantern with me and after looking round found the flags untouched, but as I stood in the center of the large hall, I heard a footfall which sounded as coming from the room to the left of the hall, as you enter. It was a light step, such as a slippered foot would cause. I stood and listened for a few seconds, expecting to see someone come from this room. As no one appeared I advanced to enter. The footfalls then sounded more distant and were evidently retreating. I stepped into the room and raised the lantern so that I could see all parts of the interior. To my great astonishment I beheld — an empty room. I stood in the center of this apartment, and believe me or not, I heard the same footfalls sounding in the large room which I had just left. I marched the castle from roof to basement and found nothing to which I could attribute the cause of this mysterious noise.

I felt easier when I emerged from the castle. Whether this occurs at other times I can't say; I haven't visited the place since and am quite willing to allow Mr. Ghost to have full possession at such an untimely hour of the night.

E. C.

To this day, the identity of the lady in blue remains a mystery. John Arctanger identified the ghost as Princess Olga Feodorovna, while other writers argue she was the niece of Adolph Etolin or the daughter of Baron Ferdinand von Wrangell. Correspondence in the Russian Archives, dated September 23, 1833, refers to the tragic love triangle A letter mentions a young officer named Paul Borusof who died under mysterious circumstances. Implicated in his death was a Colonel Bouikof.

On March 17, 1894, a fire of undetermined origin destroyed Baranof's Castle. Witnesses claimed it broke out in the cupola and spread rapidly throughout the building. Apparently the hauntings then ceased. But in August of 1987, at the newly renovated Russian Bishop's House in Sitka, a ghostly woman wearing Russian dress was seen during a conference about Russian America. Perhaps Sitka's phantom princess has returned.

Many strange tales have been told about the seas of the North Pacific and the brave men who have sailed them. But the saga of the Eliza Anderson's *final voyage ranks among the great unsolved mysteries of the Pacific Coast. The principals in this account were well-known mariners whose biographies were included in* Lewis and Dryden's History of the Pacific Northwest. *The harbor and abandoned cannery referred to in the narrative were located on Thin Point at the entrance of Cold Bay on the Alaska Peninsula. This account of the* Eliza Anderson *and her ghostly pilot was originally published in the* Seattle Post-Intelligencer *on December 12, 1899.*

The Last Voyage
of the *Eliza Anderson*

On the bleak, wind-blown shores of Alaska, not far from Dutch Harbor, lies the wreck of a once-proud steamer. Faded by months of rain and sleet, the letters which years ago gleamed black on her wheelhouse are now scarcely discernable a hundred yards away. Looking closely, one can make out the words:

"ELIZA ANDERSON"

In the summer of 1897, she had 120 souls aboard on their way to the Klondike gold fields. Their escape from death in the icy waters of the Gulf of Alaska was miraculous. The true story of that escape, and of the mystic hand that intervened between the *Anderson* and death, has never been told.

74

Crew members will vouch for the facts. They are men who laugh at ghosts, but who were with the *Anderson* on her dying day. They are convinced that the ship was saved by a supernatural being. This is the story of the *Anderson's* last voyage.

On August 10, 1897, the *Anderson* sailed from Seattle with 120 men and women aboard. In tow was the schooner *W. J. Bryant* and the old *Politofsky*, once a gunboat owned by Russia, but which was included in the sale of Alaska.

Two weeks after the ship left port she ran into one of the worst storms recorded off the Gulf of Alaska. The wind came with a velocity of forty to fifty miles per hour from the south, with waves cresting at thirty feet. The *Anderson* was at the mercy of the elements. Each towering wave hit the steamer with deadly force. The old side-wheeler fought to stay afloat, but the pounding had opened her seams, and she was taking on water.

It rained in torrents, and the barometer fell rapidly. The storm grew in violence. The *Bryant* and the old *Politofsky* broke free and were lost in the blackness that lay astern.

The battered *Anderson*, nearly out of coal, lay 250 miles from Dutch Harbor, the nearest port. The chief engineer, Bob Turner, after surveying the coal bins, determined that the ship had only ten to twelve hours of fuel left. Turner sent word to Captain Powers. A meeting of the officers was called in the captain's quarters.

Captain Powers confirmed what the officers already knew: the *Eliza Anderson* could not survive the storm. She was old and breaking apart. The captain's decision was to try to make land and beach the *Anderson* in an attempt to save the passengers.

He did not know his exact location because the storm had blown the ship off course, but he calculated they were about thirty miles off shore. If the *Anderson* lost power before she was beached, she would be wrecked in the surf. It was a gamble, but it was the only chance left.

The captain ordered the lifeboats stocked with food and blankets, but in his heart he knew the lifeboats could never survive the raging seas. He shook hands with his officers, made his way to the bridge, and took over the wheel.

Suddenly, a man appeared in the wheelhouse, clad in weather-beaten oilskins. An air of mystery hung about the stranger. He did not give his name. Determining the plight of the steamer, he pointed toward the land and said:

"There is an anchorage and an abandoned cannery at Thin Point, with coal in plenty under one of its sheds. I'll pilot you there."

Some unexplained impulse on the part of Captain Powers caused him to surrender the wheel to the stranger.

The storm had abated somewhat, but the *Anderson* was still fighting heavy seas and taking on water. Passengers stuffed rags and blankets in leaking seams in an effort to seal any leaks. The crew manned the pumps for twelve straight hours.

By the time the *Anderson* rounded Thin Point, her coal bunkers had been scraped clean, and all the furniture, bunks, any other inflammable objects, had been thrown into the firebox.

When she dropped anchor, her side-wheels made one final revolution and ground to a stop. Everyone on board breathed a prayer of thankfulness.

Beneath the wrecked roof of the abandoned

cannery, the officers of the *Anderson* found seventy-five tons of coal, preserved from the weather as if by the act of Providence. When the storm passed, temporary repairs were made. The ship then headed for Dutch Harbor.

Upon arrival, revenue officers came and surveyed the *Eliza Anderson*. They saw the gaping seams in her hull and ordered that she proceed no farther. There she lay, her anchors set in the soft sand of the harbor. A month later, a gale from the southeast drove the *Anderson* onto the rocks.

Who was the man who led the *Anderson* to a safe anchorage? He disappeared as the *Anderson* approached the shore, as if he had dropped from the clouds and ascended again.

However, one sailor who was on the *Anderson* believes the stranger was a ghost.

"It was Tom Wright's spirit," he said. "The old man was her captain for many years, and he loved the *Anderson*. He knew of her peril and came to guide her to a port of safety. Without that fuel we would have been stranded in Cold Bay. God knows how many of us would have been left to tell the story. Captain Tom's spirit saw our danger and brought us safely to land."

H. O. Blankenship was one of the original discoverers of gold on Candle Creek near Goodhope Bay. This new El Dorado was approximately 300 miles north of Nome. Blankenship became rich from his claims, but the real story lies in his account of the supernatural events that led to his discovery of gold, as told by the Nome Nugget *on September 7, 1901.*

Guided by a Ghost

H. O. Blankenship, one of the discoverers of gold on Candle Creek, a tributary to the Kiwalik, tells a story that would make an interesting chapter in a novel. Mr. Blankenship has been in Alaska four years. He made a stake in the Atlin District, but this is his first strike in northwestern Alaska. And withal, he is modest in his estimate of the value of his find, simply saying he has found good prospects.

But the story is in the circumstances and experiences that led to the discovery. Before proceeding on the trip, he consulted Mrs. Nagel, a well-known psychic of Nome, who directed him to three places, one of which was on the Kiwalik where the strike was located.

He started north on June 9 in a twenty-foot dory and was accompanied by another man as far as Cape Prince of Wales. That point was reached on June 27, and the balance of the journey was made alone, although he maintains that during the most perilous

78

days of the trip, his deceased father-in-law was constantly with him and helped him steer the boat through narrow channels of floating, grinding ice.

"When I left Nome," said Mr. Blankenship, "the ice still clung to the shore, extending in places several miles into the Bering Sea. We kept out pretty well, sometimes encountering ice which we steered through without mishap. I left Cape Prince of Wales on June 27 and did not reach the mouth of the Kugruk River until July. I encountered a great deal of ice and was carried by currents thirty or forty miles out to sea. My first realization that I was drifting out in the Arctic Ocean was the sight of a whale that came up near the boat. I knew by steering in an easterly direction I would reach land, but the sail was of little value, as there was no wind to speak of.

"The floating ice made it necessary to keep wide awake and on the alert. There was danger of being nipped. It was during this part of the voyage and for eight days that my father-in-law was with me constantly. I could see him plainly, as I saw him in life. He would sit in the bow of the boat, and by a motion of the hand would indicate how I should steer. His directions piloted me through some tight places. I never got into a place when there was danger of being nipped — and there were plenty of them — without seeing the old gentleman in the bow on lookout, quietly motioning in the direction I was to go.

"Twice during these eight days, I found favorable conditions so that I tied to an ice flow and slept, but nearly all the time it was constant vigil and hard pulling, especially in crossing the currents.

"When I reached land it was at the mouth of the

Kugruk River. I found friends there, and after taking some food, slept for sixteen hours. I went on to the Kiwalik and arrived on Candle Creek on July 26. There were two men on the creek when I got there, but they were out of provisions. I prospected the creek for eighteen miles, found gold, and staked thirty-three claims, remaining on the stream until August 23."

Discoveries of gold were obviously big news in the Northland at the turn of the century. In its September 9, 1903, issue, the Nome Nugget *reported the discovery of a huge gold nugget with a story headlined: "FOUND $3,285.90 NUGGET." Yet the story behind the nugget's discovery was not told until years later. This account of the "phantom nugget" appeared in the* Alaska-Yukon Magazine *in July of 1909.*

Unlike many stories of the time, which were often told by questionable sources, the witnesses to this strange event were prominent Alaskans. Lafe Spray was a newspaper man, miner, and court official. Ike Powers, Frank Grimm, and James O'Brien were listed as Nome miners in the 1903 Polk's Directory. The author of the Alaska-Yukon Magazine *article, A. Saverdo, commented: "The story of the vision may be substantiated by communicating with Mr. Grimm, who is now principal of Nome High School, and with Mr. Spray, who lives in Seattle."*

The Golden Vision
of Anvil Creek

The biggest gold nugget ever found in Alaska was taken from an Anvil Creek bench claim in 1903 by the Pioneer Mining Company. This claim was located by a man named Rock, who died in 1900, his widow succeeding to the ownership of the claim. She entered into a contract with Frank Grimm and Ike Powers, agreeing to give them a one-half interest in the claim if they would develop it.

81

Accordingly a small ditch was dug to the spring, and the process of sluicing off the surface earth was begun in one corner of the claim near the railroad track. One of the men employed in this project was Lafe Spray.

One day Mrs. Powers came out to the claim from her home in town and, calling Mr. Spray from his work, pointed to a certain spot and said, "Lafe, I wish you would dig there."

He asked why, and she said that the previous day at her home in town she had a curious experience — a vision, she called it.

In this vision she saw herself standing on the depot platform of the Wild Goose Railroad (the place where she was now talking to Mr. Spray) and a strange man appeared. This man walked out to where she had designated and stopped; turning on his heels with military precision and bearing, he walked back toward Mrs. Powers and approaching her asked:

"Did you notice where I stopped?"

"Yes."

"Well, under my feet at that point is a large nugget, and when this nugget is found it will prove to be the largest nugget ever found in Alaska." And then he vanished.

When she finished telling her experience, Mr. Spray said:

"The nugget may be there. I hope it is, but I will have an awfully hard time squaring myself with Ike and Grimm if I waste time picking down through the frozen clay. Why don't you get Ike to dig for it?"

"He and Grimm just laughed at me. I wish I were a man. I would get it — I just know it is there."

In 1901, Mrs. Rock sold her half of the claim to

Jimmy O'Brien. The claim became the property of Grimm, Powers, and O'Brien.

During the summer of 1902, the new owners operated in a small way, but taking out considerable gold. The following winter O'Brien continued working the claim. He announced it was his intention to find Mrs. Powers' phantom nugget. However, he was unsuccessful.

In 1903, the Powers family, having considerable sickness, was anxious to sell, and so the claim became the property of the Pioneer Mining Company. Immediately, they commenced operations on a large scale.

The Powers family sailed for California and many friends went down to see them off. A few who had heard of the vision jokingly asked Mrs. Powers if she were satisfied to go away and leave that nugget still sleeping in the cold, cold ground.

"Laugh all you like, but remember what I say, that nugget will be turned up someday — don't forget."

A few weeks later when Mr. Spray came into Nome from the hills he found the town bubbling with excitement. Nome had once more become famous by producing the largest nugget from the gravels in the Northland.

Spray was hailed on the street with:

"Have you seen it?"

"Seen what?"

"Why, the nugget, of course. It's as large as a loaf of bread and it's worth more than $3,000."

On being informed the nugget was found on the Anvil Creek bench claim, Spray remembered Mrs. Powers' vision. He was curious to find out exactly where the nugget was dug. He went out to the creek, and one of the miners showed him. It was the exact spot Mrs. Powers had seen in the vision.

During the previous winter, the partners had worked within six feet of the big nugget. One more day's work would have brought Grimm, O'Brien, and the Powers family fame and fortune. But fate had decreed otherwise.

Tagish Lake is located south of Whitehorse near the Yukon-British Columbia border. It is a large lake approximately thirty miles long, and together with Lake Bennett and Lake Marsh it forms the headwaters of the Yukon River. During the gold rush these lakes were the gateway into the Klondike gold fields.

The story of the vision on Tagish Lake, dateline Syracuse, New York, appeared in the June 24, 1916, issue of the Nome Daily Nugget. *This suggests that Ethel Williams or someone in her family gave Don Mack's letter to the wire service. As for Don Mack, there is no further record of him or his vision.*

Warning on Tagish Lake

During the Klondike gold rush, Miss Ethel Williams of Syracuse, New York, received a postcard with a strange message. The card was sent from Don Mack of Juneau, Alaska, a wealthy mining engineer.

Miss Williams, who resided with her father and sister, received a picture of a dog team and the following words in a masculine hand: "If you will write to this address, I will tell you why I have sent this card."

Intrigued, Ethel Williams responded, and later received the following account from Don Mack.

Dear Miss Williams,

I am a mining engineer and my work has taken me far into the interior of Canada and Alaska. Ordinarily I finish my work and reach the settlements before the lakes and rivers close and am able to make the trips by boats and canoes. Last fall, I delayed too long and was obliged to come out by sled, a distance of 700 miles. Shortly before I reached Tagish Lake, I fell in with three Indians and a Frenchman on the trail. We started to cross Tagish Lake, stopping midway on a small island to camp. While I slept, I dreamed that I saw a young girl dressed in light summer clothing standing in the deep snow around me. She was so real to me that I asked her who she was and why she was there.

The vision told me her name was Ethel Williams, and her home was in Syracuse, New York. She said she knew it was my intention to keep on the direct route over the lake. However, disaster lay in that direction, as there was open water covered by thin ice and snow. To be safe, I should go up the river twenty-five miles, where I would find solid ice.

At this point, I was awakened by the howling of dogs and the shouts of the Indians. It was three o'clock in the morning, and my companions were preparing to leave. I told them of my dream, but they laughed at me.

I did not go with them. I followed the instructions of the dream girl, and when I reached Skagway, the Indians and the Frenchman had not been seen. I headed a search party down the lake to the point where they should have reached the mainland. We found the canoes and some of their outfit floating in the open water.

So, Miss Williams, I consider that you saved my life, and mailed this card to you from Juneau.

Most ghost stories describe spirits as haunting particular places — an old hotel, a former home, even a favorite ship. The following story is unusual because the ghost haunted the trail to Tiekel City, but never frequented the roadhouse or any other dwelling. Tiekel City, located along the Tiekel River and what is now the Richardson Highway, burned in 1898 and the site was abandoned. A roadhouse was built across from the camp, and this was the establishment Charlie Romer operated at the time of the ghostly manifestations. This story appeared originally in the October 20, 1933, edition of the Alaska Weekly.

The Searching Maiden of Tiekel City

The ghost appears almost every night just after dusk and follows a well-defined route down the hill toward Tiekel City. It carries a lighted lamp or lantern and at times seems to pause and carefully search for some object.

The apparition has been sighted by five different persons, including Charlie Romer, proprietor of the Tiekel Roadhouse. He swears he has seen the manifestation six times. It appears on the hillside opposite the roadhouse, and above the site of the ancient stampede camp of Tiekel City.

When the apparition was first seen, the roadhouse people thought some traveler had wandered off the trail and was coming to the roadhouse for the night. But when no one showed up, they were at a loss for an explanation and made the trip up the hill where the light had last been seen. To their surprise they found no tracks or evidence of anyone having passed that way and decided that possibly they might have been mistaken. The next night, however, the apparition again appeared, covering the same route and again carrying a light. This time three people assert that they saw the light, but the next morning's search again failed to reveal any track.

The following night two prospectors made the trip up the hill and cached themselves alongside the route that had been followed by the ghost on the two previous nights, but while they failed to see anything unusual, the party at the roadhouse again saw the mysterious light moving down the same trail.

There is simply no explanation for the strange appearance, and old-timers are digging up tales of the past in an effort to solve the mystery that has the whole countryside talking.

One of the tales is that the apparition is the ghost of an Indian maiden who in the days of the Klondike rush fell in love with a young miner from the Black Hills. He had camped at Tiekel City on his way into the Yukon, waiting for the trails to freeze over. In the brief time he was there, he completely won the heart of an Indian girl. When the trail was passable, he moved on toward the distant gold fields, leaving the girl behind, but promising to come back for her. For a time she hopefully waited for his return. But when winter set in again and he did not return, she began to look for him up on the hill where he had pitched his tent. Often she walked the trail with a lantern to guide her miner back to their camp.

One night she was caught in a blizzard and perished. Old-timers claim that her ghost still haunts the hill, looking for the handsome young prospector who won her heart.

Lost Mines

Wherever prospectors gathered, tales were told of fabulously rich mines that were lost and never found again. In most stories, the unlucky prospector, driven away by hostile Natives or forced to return to civilization for provisions, never returned to his mine. Or, if he attempted to return, he was so weak from hunger or wounds that he became confused, unable to locate his claim. In some accounts, the miner left behind a rude map which no one else was able to understand.

Most lost mine stories were will o'-the-wisp yarns told by lonely men around campfires long dead. But not all were simple yarns. Some of the stories were supported by surprising evidence, such as ore samples, assay reports, and pokes of nuggets and coarse gold.

One of the richest deposits of gold ever discovered in North America may lie somewhere in the St. Elias Mountain Range along the upper Yukon River. This mountain range is 300 miles long and ninety miles wide, extending northwest along the Alaska-Canada boundary from Cross Sound to Cape Yakataga, a largely unexplored wilderness of glaciers, mountains, and forests. During gold rush times this was the territory of the fierce Yakutat Indians, a subtribe of the Tlingits. It was probably the Yakutats who attacked the prospecting party in the following story, printed in the February 1921 edition of the Pathfinder, *a publication of the Alaska-Yukon Pioneers.*

The Golden Bar

Probably the most interesting tale of lost mines of Alaska is the Lake with the Golden Bar, the richest of all rich mines lost to the world.

In August of 1884, three prospectors — Galt, Ulrich, and Ole Stanford — crossed the St. Elias Range near the Yukon River. One evening they came upon a small lake. The evening sunlight, shining full upon a bar in the lake but a few feet from the shore, glittered a thousand golden rays. A hasty examination showed the bar to be literally paved with golden nuggets. Throwing down their rifles and packs, the men plunged into the water and swam to the bar. The first nugget they picked up weighed about ten pounds. Then Ulrich secured one which weighed all of fifty pounds.

For several weeks the three prospectors remained at the lake, picking out the golden nuggets and stowing them away in a cave nearby. Soon they had accumulated half a ton or more of the precious metal. They also built a small cabin, intending to winter near the lake. But hostile Indians attacked them, killing Stanford and burning the cabin. Galt and Ulrich escaped the Indians, but in doing so became separated, and, destitute of provisions, started for civilization. After much suffering, they succeeded in reaching the coast and eventually the States.

Galt became paralyzed as a result of the hardships he had undergone during the fearful trip to the coast. But the next year Ulrich started for Alaska to recover the gold the party had accumulated. He was never heard of again. His fate remains a mystery.

The story of the discovery of a gold deposit, or "placer," at a Crescent Lake somewhere in the Stikine River country is one of the best-documented lost mine accounts in Alaska. The principals in this story were well-known Alaskans. Dr. O. W. Stanton was a physician in Wrangell in the late 1890s and early 1900s, listed in the 1902 Polk's Directory as a druggist and physician. Calvin Barkdull, a miner, testified to seeing the mint receipt for $5,000 (at $18 per ounce of gold) that Dr. Stanton had obtained from a dying prospector, proving that the man had located a rich placer. In 1936, Barkdull related his story to a group of Alaska-Yukon Pioneers. The Alaska Weekly for February 14, 1936, published his account.

Map to Crescent Lake

Calvin H. Barkdull was an early prospector in Southeastern Alaska. In the winter of 1894, in company with Jim Greenslate and Sam Gowen, he pulled into Wrangell, Alaska, from the Unuk River stampede. At that time there were no maps or charts of Alaska. Wrangell was the only post south of Juneau that boasted of a few pilings to which the monthly steamer *The City of Topeka* could tie up.

While Barkdull was looking over the town, his attention was drawn to a collection of garnets and gold ore in the window of Dr. Stanton's drugstore. He went in and discussed mines and mining with the doctor. After the doctor had asked him a number of questions of rather a personal nature, he was

94

invited into the doctor's office and told the following tale:

"In the late eighties I was operating a hospital and following my profession as doctor and surgeon in the East. One day a man came into my office suffering from an old gunshot wound in the lung. I took him to my hospital, but in spite of my best medical attention he grew weaker and failed to recover.

"Before he passed away he told me that in company with another white man, an Indian, and an Indian woman, he had once left Sitka, Alaska, in an Indian canoe and traveled four days to the mouth of a river that emptied into what is now known as Frederick Sound.

"After two days of poling and lining the canoe up the river, they came to a small clear stream which flowed into the river from the south. From there the trail followed up the small stream to a crescent-shaped lake with a tiny island in the center. From a small stream emptying into the lake on the north side is where they mined about $17,000 worth of gold.

"A dispute arose in regard to the division of the gold which led to a shooting affray and the death of the Indian and one white man, and the wounding of himself in the left breast. The Indian woman ran away and hid in the woods. He took his share of the gold, went to the canoe, floated down the river, was picked up off Cape Fanshaw by the cutter *Pinta*, and taken to the Marine Hospital at Port Townsend, Washington. After several weeks he was well enough to go east, and there he was."

Barkdull continued the story: "Dr. Stanton brought out a much-worn map from his desk and showed it to me, saying, 'This is the map he gave me before he passed away, and here are mint receipts for about $5,000. With this evidence in hand I disposed of my eastern interests, moved to Wrangell, and have spent three years looking for that mine but have not been able to find it. I found the Indian that had escaped from the party alive. She told me that under penalty of death from other Indians she must not reveal the location.' With that he concluded, saying, 'Now go out and find that mine and stake me in on it.'"

Since that time, Barkdull has prospected and explored every river in Southeastern Alaska — the Unuk, Stikine, Taku, Whiting, Farragut — and many lakes. But the Crescent Lake placer still waits to make some prospector rich beyond his wildest dreams.

Every mining camp in the West had a lost rocker story. This was understandable, as a rocker, a small gold recovery device, was a common item found at every placer site. Yet often when miners left a rocker at a good site, on returning they could find neither the site nor the rocker.

Of all the "lost rocker" stories, this is the best documented. Prospectors persistently searched for the Lost Rocker Mine in Southeast Alaska for decades. From the time of the original strike in the 1870s through World War II, they outfitted nearly every spring in hopes of locating the fabulously rich placer. The earliest known account of this Lost Rocker appeared in the December 6, 1899, edition of the Alaska Mining Record.

The Lost Rocker

In the year 1867, Captain Lewis of the Hudson Bay Company, while on a cruise on the steamer *Otter*, picked up a drifting canoe in the vicinity of Taku Harbor. The canoe contained the almost lifeless body of Fred Culver, a prospector. He was cared for by the captain. On gaining sufficient strength, Culver told his tragic story. He told how he and two partners had been out prospecting on adjacent islands. They located marvelously rich placer mines on a beautiful stream that emptied into a lake. While working on their claim they were attacked by Indians, who killed his two partners and seriously wounded Culver.

He was taken to Port Townsend, where he told

his story of the discovery of the new diggings, and said he could direct a party to them. A number of men immediately outfitted and started in search of the spot where Culver's friends had met their tragic death.

On arriving in Alaskan waters, Culver's mind seemed to wander, and he was unable to locate the strike. His companions became angry and threatened his life because they thought he was deceiving them. But Culver was sincere that he could not relocate the placer mines, and his partners took him to Sitka, where he soon died. To this date, the river which is said to flow over a bed of yellow metal has not been found, although several prospectors claimed to have had leads to the location of the Lost Rocker.

The following letter was written on September 16, 1868, and appeared in the Alaska Weekly *on December 30, 1932. James Little, an Alaska-Yukon prospector, gave the letter to the newspaper and vouched for its authenticity. For some reason, the editor of the* Alaska Weekly *refused to reveal the name of the letter-writer, stating: "We cannot at this time disclose the names of the brothers concerned in the letter set out in this story. . . ."*

Mountain of Fire

Fort Wrangell, Alaska

Sept. 16, 1868
Dear Brother:

I was off hunting with a party of Indians from the vicinity of the fort. We were in camp about twenty miles inland from Wrangell when an Indian ran into the circle of firelight, his teeth chattering and his face fairly gray with terror. When he calmed down, he told the following story. He said his name was Peeochcc, or in the white man's tongue, "The Fox." He had left the village a week before on a trapping expedition. While at work among his traps he had accidentally run onto the line set by a wandering party of Tak-heesh Natives from the interior and had ignorantly — so he assured us again and again — taken several pelts from their traps.

A dozen Tak-heesh had suddenly come upon

him, taken him prisoner, and vowed he should die for the offense.

Poor Peeschee in vain asserted his innocence, but his captors bound him to a tree. On the second day of his captivity he had escaped by gnawing his thongs while his captors were dozing after a hearty meal of bear meat, and he had been running all the afternoon, he said.

We felt a little nervous about the pursuers, but these Tak-heesh are cowards unless they are terribly aroused, and, sure enough, when they turned up the next morning a rifle volley poured into the air put the whole crowd to flight. Peeschee was grateful, and the day after we reached Fort Wrangell he did me the good turn I referred to.

He came quietly to the quarters, inquired for my room, found me alone, and then and there, told me the wonderful story which set me to writing this long letter — an offense, Brother, which I seldom commit, you'll acknowledge.

What Peeschee had to say is substantially this: Last autumn he made one of his solitary expeditions over the mountains in search of furs. He penetrated far into the interior, reaching a district absolutely unknown to him before that trip. He describes it as abounding in game and heavily wooded. There were many rapid streams, all seeming to be well stocked with trout, grayling, and other fish. As often occurs in Alaska, the weather was cloudy for fully ten days at a stretch.

He wandered ahead and toward the close of a dull, drizzly afternoon, Peeschee stopped for the night on the bank of a swift brook. Suddenly the clouds in the west began to break away, and, as they gradually parted, there appeared, high in the heavens, what seemed to be a mountain of fire. It was soft, glowing crimson and from its summit arose a huge column of smoke. Peeschee had never set eyes on it before in his life. It was beyond doubt a mountain peak. Within five minutes the clouds had closed in again and the wonderful peak was shut out from view.

The next three days he spent in traveling straight uphill toward this mountain. After much struggling through jungles and morasses, fording streams and encountering wild beasts by day and night, he claims that he reached the base of the peak and discovered the cause of its strange color. He brought a piece of the live rock itself and showed it to me. I have it on my desk now. It has been examined by Haley, the ex-soldier and prospector, and he says it is a magnificent specimen of cinnabar, deep crimson in color, promising, Haley says, to yield, if worked, an enormous percentage of weight of pure metal.

Brother, that was a mountain of cinnabar . . . of mercury. It waits for someone to take those red heaps of granite and quartz, fuse them, and bear away a fortune as you could not make in a century of prosperous mill operations at your New England plant. Will you come? Just you, Haley, and I are in on it. Just we three. Will you come?

This is what I propose. You have been in indifferent health for some time. You need a change. You could leave a competent superintendent in charge of your mills back there.

You always liked hunting and camping out. Take the boys along and meet me at Wrangell, then we can proceed together to this mountain of cinnabar and make a rough survey, lay out our claims, and start real work the following spring. In other words you can start out as soon as spring of 1869 dawns and reach Wrangell in plenty of time to spend several months on the property and finish all our prospecting. We should then be ready to take out ore the following May.

One more point to consider and then I am done. It is, I admit, an important point. How shall we find this half-fabulous mountain after we have effected a union of forces at Wrangell?

Here we must rely entirely on the Indian, Peeschee. He proposes to start from the fort and strike due southeast. After traveling three hundred miles straight into the wilderness, Peeschee says we shall find ourselves at the foot of a lofty range of mountains. From this point he bears away slightly to the east, and within three or four days, expects to reach his old camping ground from which he obtained his first view of the flaming peak. Then will begin by far our hardest fight with the forces of nature.

Peeschee has drawn a map which he claims to understand, and by which he proposes to follow — as nearly as possible — his former route to the base of the mountain and up its steep sides. I have borrowed this map or chart and will trace it here for you. It's a curious-looking affair, but with Peeschee as guide, I'd stake it against a government chart. Every mark on it means something to him. I'll give you his explanation at some other time.

Now then, once more — WILL YOU COME?

Your affectionate brother,
John

In a follow-up letter to the Alaska Weekly, published on February 3, 1932, James Little claimed the brothers located the cinnabar deposit and sold the property to a San Francisco firm, but the company never worked the claim due to its isolated location.

Somewhere in the Stikine River country lies a rich placer that has passed into history as the Valley of Gold. Maybe it should instead be called the "Valley of Death," after all the prospectors who have died attempting to locate it. Some may have died at the hands of the Tlingits, the original discoverers of the rich gravels. The Tlingits knew the value of their mine, and their penalty for trespassing was death.

The following story appeared in the Stroller's Weekly *on July 21, 1928, and is one of the best-documented accounts of a lost Native mine.*

The Valley of Gold

The Valley of Gold has been the object of constant search since the days of Russian occupancy. It has been the rainbow dream of old prospectors, and dozens of lives have been laid down in a fruitless search for it.

Tales of the valley were first recorded by the Russian government which formerly occupied Alaska. In those days, Indians arrived at Sitka, the capital, with pockets and pouches bulging with gold nuggets and flakes.

The Indians spent freely and boasted of having an unlimited source. The Russians obtained the gold from the Indians by selling them trade goods. The Indians would disappear and return a few weeks later with pouches bulging with nuggets.

Reports of the fabulous wealth reached the ears of the czar, and he ordered that a concentrated search be made for the valley. The Indians soon lost the scouts, who reported that the Indians had gone in canoes up the Stikine River.

A detachment of Russian soldiers was detailed to search the headwaters of the Stikine River, but they never returned.

The valley was next reported about 1898. Indians appeared at Wrangell with a large supply of gold nuggets and flakes. They went on a wild spending spree and drank too much hooch. From their unguarded talk, one prospector determined the general location of the mine. He returned to Wrangell several months later with a heavy poke of gold. He described the gold as being in mounds at the foot of a glacier in an inland valley. The miner organized an expedition to go in again, and was never more heard of.

Years later, the McLode brothers found the Valley of Gold. According to their report, they were the first white men to enter the valley. Charlie McLode's account:

"Here is the queer thing that we first found," says the survivor of the ill-fated trip of the first white men to see the mine.

"Although the Indians had left their pans and shovels right where they had been working, and their campsites were there, too, there wasn't a single sign of fire."

Apparently the Indians had never lit fires there, taking in supplies of jerked meat, so that no telltale smoke would betray the secret of the gold to some wandering white.

For three months the McLodes worked the mine, taking out gold. They left the valley to buy supplies to carry them through the winter. For some reason,

Charlie was not with his brothers, Billy and Frank, when they returned to the mine. They were never seen alive again. Charlie searched for his brothers and, from information supplied by the Indians, found their bones. They had been murdered and robbed of the gold. Somehow Charlie found out who killed his brothers and apparently administered vigilante justice. In an interview, he stated:

"They were not murdered by Indians; they were murdered by a white man. I know who that man was, but he is dead now. Little good the gold he stole ever did him."

Charlie McLode never returned to the golden valley, nor did he reveal its location. He said the valley had taken enough lives already. Charlie took the location to his grave.

The following account, as it appeared in the Daily Alaska Dispatch for November 15, 1912, was related by Allison French, an early-day prospector. French is somewhat vague about the geography of the Porcupine-Mackenzie River country — which is understandable, as the country had not been mapped and was still largely unexplored. French placed the prospectors in Alaska when they were probably in the Yukon, but they may have been as far east as the Northwest Territories. The editor commented: "That the story is given more or less credence by prospectors of the North is shown by the fact that there are experienced men willing to look for the rich but mysterious stream."

A Creek Lined with Gold

It is not often that old prospectors go hunting for lost deposits, but now and then they do. Three of them have recently left Fairbanks for the fabled bed of nuggets underlying one of the tributaries of the Porcupine River.

The story of the found and lost treasure is best told by Allison French, who says that twelve years ago four men were camped on the upper Porcupine River, about 400 miles beyond Rampart. It was their purpose to prospect the next season on the headwaters of certain tributaries of the Mackenzie, which rises to a low range of mountains northwesterly from the site of their camp.

In February there came a spell of weather quite

exceptional in that part of Alaska, the snow packed down hard and frozen, making it possible to travel by dog team rapidly and with ease. The four men loaded their teams with food and supplies and mushed north.

They crossed the low mountain range and found a level country across which they made rapid progress in four or five days, then reached a creek which puts into the Mackenzie River. They cut holes into the ice and panned the creek. The pay was fair and they devoted several days to the work.

Presently one of the prospectors named Johnson grew dissatisfied and left his companions for a prospecting trip down the stream. He had gone but a few miles when he was startled to find in a piece of "anchor ice" a handful of gravel and a good-sized gold nugget.

Johnson cut a hole in the ice in the middle of the stream. There were several feet of water, flowing swiftly, but he could plainly see the gravel on the bottom. And mingled with the gravel he saw something that nearly took his breath away. The bottom was thickly sown with large gold nuggets.

How to get the gold puzzled him for a while, but he made a crude tool from willow saplings and was able to secure the nuggets one by one.

Before he returned to camp, he cached the gold. He was a greedy man and did not tell his companions of his startling discovery.

Johnson often prospected by himself and his partners thought nothing about it when Johnson would take off for several days. Johnson returned to the creek and worked it until he had all the gold he could carry. He then made some excuse and left for the Outside. It is estimated that he carried 250 pounds of nuggets.

He made his way to Chicago and deposited the gold in a safety deposit box. He planned to return to the Mackenzie River country and his creek for more gold and decided to take a Chicago friend named Brown. He told his friend the story of the bed of nuggets and made a map of the country, pledging Brown to secrecy.

But Johnson died of a disease he had contracted in the North and Brown secured another partner (name unknown). They reached the Porcupine country late in the year and found a morass where Johnson had found a field of snow. They went around the swampy land.

Then Brown's partner became discouraged and returned to the Outside. Brown secured another partner and went back the following winter. They were never heard from again.

In the North Country there are many places that some Natives have believed to be haunted. In this particular account, the haunting incident may have been fabricated by the prospectors to confirm the Natives' belief that the place was "bad medicine," and consequently keep them and other prospectors out of the area.

The story takes place in the Similkameen country, which is approximately 150 miles east of Vancouver, British Columbia. The town of Princeton, at the junction of the Similkameen and Tulameen Rivers, served as the center of mining and agriculture in the district in the early 1900s. Related by Judge Thomas C. Murphy, the following account was first published in the Similkameen Star *and then reprinted on January 22, 1901, in the* Semi-Weekly World, *a Vancouver, B.C., newspaper.*

The Haunted Mine

In the summer of 1850, a party of prospectors from the south came up the Similkameen River and went into the mountains at the head of the river, where they remained all summer, returning in the fall. They showed very rich gold specimens to a man named Walker, who at the time was the only white settler on the Similkameen River. They told Walker that they had struck a rich gold quartz ledge.

The next year they came again, with a much larger party and a big pack train. They went north as before but have never been seen nor heard from again.

Until a short time ago no one had ever located the golden ledge again. Had it not been for an Indian woman, it might never have been found.

This woman was the wife of a "remittance man" named Horace Parker Manley, who was nicknamed "Parkey." He had a friend, Mike Widrow, who had a homestead nearby. It was at a time when the grass was so short that both families were living on roots, that Parkey's [wife] told that her grandfather used to boast that he knew where the white man's golden ledge was, and also to hint in a vague way of knowing what became of the white men who found it.

The information fired the mining instinct of Widrow. There were possibilities in it for grub and whiskey, and Mike used to say that "if it panned out all right, they could buy enough rum to float a ship." The younger Indians also became excited about the prospect of lots of potlatch, and convinced the old man to reveal the location of the mine. The grandfather scratched a map on the ground showing where the ledge was located. The Indians knew the general area, but the mine was located in an area that they considered "bad medicine." The Indians guided Manley and Widrow to a small creek, an affluent of the Tulameen River. They refused to go any farther, as they said the place was guarded by evil spirits. The [wife's] grandfather had given them directions on how to get to the mine from where the Indians had camped on the creek. The white men were to follow the creek up to a small bench covered with white rocks. A cabin had been built on the bench at one time, but it had been burned. After the cabin site they were to look directly across the creek and they would see a hole in the mountain — that was the place.

Parkey and Mike had little trouble in finding the mine. The mouth of the old tunnel had caved in and the debris from the mountain had covered up the old workings, yet there was a small opening by which they were able to get into the tunnel. In the entrance, Mike found a piece of quartz so rich that he couldn't believe his eyes. On striking a light and looking around, they were startled to see human bones scattered on the floor. They counted seven skulls, which showed that at least seven persons had perished there. Taking a few quartz specimens, they returned to the bench and made camp. They looked at the samples they had found and speculated how many thousands of dollars it would run to the ton.

Then they slept. How long they slept they did not know, but sometime during the night they were startled from their sleep by a yell so loud and savage that it brought them to their feet in an instant. Before they realized where the sound was coming from, it was again repeated, accompanied by Indian war cries. Then the sharp reports of rifles and pistols seemed to come from the site of the cabin. The air was filled with groans and yells; they were in the midst of a battle fought by unseen combatants. Overcome by terror, Manley and Widrow fled down the canyon. They went back to Granite, and Mike told the story in the saloon.

"Boys," he said, "I lost my clothes and came near losing my life, but I saved the pocket of my jumper." He produced the pocket and dumped the contents on the bar. There was no question of their richness. Mike told the story of how they were driven away by ghosts and how they had most of their clothes torn off in their mad flight through the bushes and rocks. But ghosts or no ghosts, the rich specimens were there to prove that they had found the rich mine, and a party was made up to return to the mine. The group was to be guided by Manley and Widrow. It included Father John, a preacher who had founded a mission in the Northwest from a land grant from the Canadian government.

For reasons not clear, Mike Widrow shot and killed Parkey Manley. The other miners took Manley back to the settlement and he was tried before Judge Baccus, better known as "Old Hang 'Em." The judge lived up to his name because in six short weeks Widrow was tried and sent to the gallows.

To the credit of Father John, be it said that he never deserted Mike Widrow but stayed with him to the end. The rest of the miners said that his only interest in Mike was to learn where the mine was located. Judge Murphy continued:

"I know this is not true, for although Father John makes excursions into the mountains each year, he always returns empty handed. Yes, the mine is still there, somewhere near a small stream that flows into the Tulameen River."

Forgotten Civilizations

Among the unsolved mysteries of the Far North are the traces of ancient civilizations uncovered by explorers or by mining operations. Miners found coins, beads, pottery, figurines, and other artifacts of ancient people under the frozen ground, at depths ranging from five to one hundred feet. One of the most puzzling discoveries occurred when the Solomon Mining Company uncovered a petrified tree stump with very unusual markings in the winter of 1909.

Several of these accounts refer to scientists who examined the finds. Some readers may find this strange, but in fact many educated people took part in the gold rush. They held degrees from universities in Europe, Canada, and the United States, and apparently a few had training in archaeology and Egyptology. These were not people likely to be victims of a hoax.

George Kershon's discovery of an ancient city in Alaska, somewhere along the Yukon River, ranks among the great unsolved mysteries of the Far North. His account of the discovery of the petrified city was originally printed in the San Francisco Examiner *and reprinted in* The Wonders of Alaska *by editor Alexander Badlam in 1891. At the end of the account, Badlam comments on the truthfulness of George Kershon.*

A City of Ice

"In the summer of 1888, I was one of the party who left here to go north prospecting. At Juneau we purchased a small sloop to take our outfit up to the Yukon, which we reached after many weeks of toil. I disagreed with my partners and engaged an Indian canoe with two Indians, and started to prospect along an unknown fork of the Yukon River. We had a terrible time. The stream narrowed in between high cliffs and shot dizzy swiftness down the gulches, making it necessary to tow the canoe by means of a line from the banks, two doing this while the other rested. Progress was necessarily slow, and many days we toiled before the first range of cliffs and mountains was passed. Once a hundred-foot waterfall barred us, and it took three days to get around it.

"After this it was a bit easier. The river broadened out and the country was more level. The banks were well wooded and game was plentiful. We kept on like this, always going north, when after six weeks a range of mountains was sighted; I believed this to be the head of the river, and pressed on to reach it before the cold weather set in. Snow was now falling very often, and it was evident that the short summer was nearly done. At length we reached the wild country again, and the stream, which had been subdividing itself into lesser ones, soon became too difficult to navigate. This was almost at the foot of the range of mountains spoken of. Here we determined to camp for the winter, and good quarters were found. Everything was made snug, as the weather up there is something awful, but we were in a deep ravine, overhung by high cliffs, which broke the fury of the winds, and the best was made of it. Game was plentiful, and large quantities of deer were shot and frozen for use through the long winter months.

"Before long the cold came, and at times it was impossible to stir from cover, especially was the case when the terrible wind blew. At other times it was fairly comfortable, although the lack of sun made it gloomy enough. Toward the end of winter it began to get light and the gales were less frequent.

"One day I determined to try and scale one of the mountains near us, as I got so tired and weary with being penned up in such a confined space. This idea I put before the Indians. One of them said he would go with me. The other one would not risk it so he was left in camp. A storm shortly arose, blowing heavily for three days, but as soon as the weather had settled, the Indian and myself started off on our trip.

"We went right up the line of the frozen river, which, being a solid mass of ice, made a good roadway. Following this for about twenty miles, at a pretty steep rise, we reached a plateau between the foothills and high range. Here the stream ended, and we started to climb one of the big hills. After a lot of hard work we reached a point near the summit. A wonderful view was had from here, but the strangest thing was a city in one of the valleys below.

"You may depend upon it, I was surprised to see it. At first I thought it was some fantastic arrangement of ice and snow which had assumed the form of a city, but examination with the glass showed that such was not the case, it being too regular in appearance. It was a city sure enough. Determined to see more of it, I commenced to work downwards, although the Indian was rather frightened, he evidently not considering it 'good medicine.'

"After several hours of hard work I reached the outskirts of this mysterious city, and found that the place was laid out in streets, with blocks of strange-looking buildings that appeared to be mosques, towers, ports, etc., and every evidence of having been built by art. The whole was not of solid ice, though it seemed to be, but blows from a hatchet on one of the walls disclosed the fact that beneath this barrier of ice was some sort of building material. It looked to be wood, but of a stone-like hardness and apparently petrified. The silence around the place was something ghostly. Not the slightest sound broke the awful stillness of the place which, added to the weird look of the empty streets, made it gruesome enough. I soon got tired of investigating the city, as the streets were blocked in many places with huge masses of ice, rendering passage almost impossible. The Indian, too, became uneasy, and we started on the return trip, reaching home the next day, tired but satisfied that we had been the first men to gaze on that silent city for centuries.

"After spring broke I made some strikes in nugget gold at the headwaters of the river, working with the Indians through the summer months, leaving camp for the Yukon about the end of August. We reached that river all right, the trip down being easy, and in due time I got back to Juneau, where I took the steamer for the south.

"It was while I was at Juneau I saw a newspaper with an account of the mirage seen at Muir Glacier. I did not make any allusions to this, though, as I did not think anyone would believe me, but I am positive that the mirage of Muir Glacier is the reflection of the frozen city found by me. In accounting for the presence of this wonderful reflected city, I'll have to leave that to abler heads. You might ask me how the ruins of big cities came to be in the interior of Central America. They are there, but who built them nobody knows. Perhaps at one time it was not so cold in the north as it is now."

This ended Mr. Kershon's story, told with an air of truth which made it evident that he had truly seen the things he said he did.

Archaeologists generally date the invention of the coin around 700 B.C., but in September of 1900, near Dawson City, in the Yukon, Henry Nicodet discovered a coin that appeared to have been minted before the Ice Age. Here is the story of that find, as reported by a Dawson newspaper and reprinted in the September 22, 1900, issue of the Daily Alaska Dispatch, *a Juneau newspaper.*

The Coin of Mystery

A remarkable coin has been found by Henry Nicodet at the head of Big Skookum Gulch and under fourteen feet of frozen earth. While mining there with two companions, Nicodet sunk to bedrock, the last five feet being through an ancient glacial mass of ice. Directly beneath the paleocrystic mass, and lying on a fold of bedrock, he found a coin that is a puzzle to the archaeologist and numismatic experts of this section, though there are men here skilled in reading Egyptian hieroglyphics and other ancient languages. It is about the size of a copper cent, though not more than half as thick, and is apparently of brass or some combination of copper and zinc. Both sides are covered with strange characters resembling hieroglyphics to the untrained eye, and the edge is milled. A peculiar thing about this coin is that it does not appear to be worn at all, the edges of the hieroglyphics being as sharp and clear-cut as a new twenty-dollar gold piece. It was made with a die like a modern coin.

The circumstances surrounding its finding are

vouched for by Nicodet and his two fellow workers, and the fact that no coin like it has ever been seen here before is a circumstance tending to confirm the story. If their statement is accepted as true, it means that prior to the glacial epoch, before the country was frozen up, the coin was washed with the gravel and sand of Big Skookum and finally found a resting place, where it was discovered many aeons of time afterwards. From that time of the Ice Age, this country has remained locked in a frozen state, the underlying muck, gravel, and broken bedrock never having thawed or become free. It is presupposed that the pre-glacial inhabitants of this country were well advanced in the arts of smelting, refining, and combining of metals; that they were sufficiently civilized to understand the construction of dies and the manufacture of coins; that they possessed a written language; and that they had passed the stage of barter and realized the need for money.

If all of this is granted, it must also be presumed that they were correspondingly advanced in other and collateral respects.

The Klondike miner digging for gold is doubtless finding traces of a once powerful and civilized race that passed away in the immeasurable depth of time, destroyed by the lowering temperatures that formed this immense ice field.

Evidences of a former race having inhabited this section are unfortunately rare, but only on a few creeks has work been done, and there only to an upper bedrock beneath which is a substratum of gravel superimposed on a second and probably primitive bedrock. When this is penetrated, additional evidence of early occupation will probably be found.

A remarkable discovery of evidence of an ancient, pre-glacial period civilization was reportedly made by William Conrad on Dewey Creek near Nome, Alaska, in 1901. This article appeared first in the Nome Nugget *and was reprinted in the* Douglas Island News *on July 14, 1909.*

The Aztec Connection

Some time ago the *Nome Nugget* published a story to the effect that a number of relics of a prehistoric race had been found below a slide of schist on Dewey Creek, a tributary of the Nome River, about twenty miles from the coast, and the narrative was read with a great deal of skepticism.

These doubts were removed yesterday when William Conrad, the man who made the discovery, brought to Nome the very things which he said he found, and he is going back in two or three days to get a number of others which have since been discovered.

All the relics are extremely interesting, and the local archaeologist and Egyptologist are having the time of their lives in offering opinions as to how they came to the place they were found, how long they have lain there, and by whom they were deposited.

These theories, offered by Dr. Chambers, S. J. Baggs, and many other scientists and near-scientists, are to the effect that they are either of local manufacture or of Egyptian or Aztec origin.

The most interesting piece is a bas-relief, about

the size of a large soup plate, in which a woman's face stands forth in bold relicf, and a number of figures appear to have been carved on the rim. There is also a bust of a man, the features of which are undoubtedly Ethiopian. The nose is long and broad at the bottom with wide nostrils, the forehead low, the hair curly, the lips thick, and the cheeks high. Another relic is an image of a falcon, a bird that is still found in Alaska today.

To a man whose sole knowledge of Egyptology and archaeology could be written on a postage stamp but who has a slight knowledge of geology and has seen a few relics in museums, it looks as though the figures might be of Aztec origin. They resemble in a small way the figures found among the ruins of South American cities today, and look as though they were made of similar material. This, however, is merely conjecture.

It is patent, however, that the person who made the bas-relief knew very little of geology, and he or she made the mistake of making or carving or molding a substance known as sesqui-oxide of iron, or sienna, and composed of oxygen and iron in the proportions of three to two, and which disintegrates rapidly when exposed to the atmosphere.

The other articles, however, look like burnt clay, and the bust bears evidence of fire treatment. It is probable that the Aztecs at one time lived in Alaska; in fact, certain scientists have brought much evidence to prove that such is the case. It is well to remember that the former occupants of this territory knew something of the art of making pottery from clay. It is probable that some aborigine of the ages long since past molded clay into the relics which are now attracting so much attention.

Miners in the Yukon made many strange discoveries while stripping off the ground's frozen muck to uncover gold-bearing gravel. Near Dawson City, along Bonanza Creek, where the first Klondike gold was discovered, one particular find suggested that Americans and Europeans were not the first miners to prospect in the Far North. In February of 1901, the Klondike Nugget *reported the discovery of a drift — a horizontal mining tunnel — dug by some ancient miner long before the Klondike strike.*

Ancient Mine Shaft

The work of sinking shafts through the muck and gravel of the creek beds in this northern country bids fair to result in more than mere contributions to the world's supply of filthy lucre. It is quite plain from events which have recently transpired that the Klondike will contribute liberally not only of its vast wealth to the arteries of trade but will also furnish information of a scientific nature which by many people will be held of even more value than the golden stream which has been pouring forth unceasingly ever since George Carmack picked up his first nugget on Bonanza Creek.

A short time ago on a tributary of Hunker Creek the remains of several mammoths were uncovered and the bones of these animals, long since extinct, are now on exhibition in Dawson.

A few days since, a discovery of equal importance was made on the upper Bonanza. This discovery involved nothing less than proof of the theory long held tenaciously by men who claim deep insight into matters prehistoric, that the placer mines of this country were known and worked in ages long since past.

An ancient drift bearing the unmistakable evidence of human workmanship has been uncovered on a hillside claim opposite Nos. 18 and 19 of the upper Bonanza, on the left limit.

Dominion Land Surveyor C. S. W. Barwell, who has just returned from the creek, gives an authority to the report which is beyond question accurate and reliable. Workmen on the claim above referred to have been drifting for some time into the face of an immense slide, which, however, bears all the evidence of having remained in its present position for untold centuries.

The tunnel which the men have been driving runs into the face of the slide, which, at the point where the ancient drift was discovered, is about 150 feet in depth. All the evidences are present in the drift to indicate that, at some time distant, mining operations had been carried on.

The ancient drift is about five feet in width and thirty feet in length and of sufficient height to enable a man to work in it. A remarkable feature of the matter is the discovery of charred wood in the drift, which indicates that the old-fashioned method of thawing was understood and practiced by the ancient miners, whoever they may have been.

Various theories have been advanced to explain the time and circumstances under which the drift was constructed, but all who are familiar with the facts agree that it must have occurred in the long, long ago — just how far they leave it to development and scientific authorities to say.

One of the most puzzling traces of an unknown civilization was part of a petrified tree stump uncovered by the Solomon Mining Company on Candle Creek near Nome, Alaska. Found one hundred feet below the frozen surface, the stump was later shipped to the Smithsonian Institution. The following article, which appeared in the Alaska-Yukon Magazine *in January of 1909, explains why.*

From the Dawn of Time

There stands on the main floor of the Smithsonian Institution in Washington, carefully enclosed in glass, an Alaskan exhibit which at first sight has a commonplace appearance. Upon investigation, the find proves to be one of the most baffling mysteries that has ever come from that vast land of the forgotten past. And in a few months this great petrified stump will be placed in a freight car and shipped across the continent to Seattle. There it will be placed in a central portion in the great Alaska building of the Alaska-Yukon-Pacific Exposition.

There does not at first seem much reason for keeping in an honored place a petrified stump. Most people have seen petrified trees, and there is no reason why they should not be found in Alaska as in other portions of the world.

But this stump is different from all others in the world. The tree which grew from its mighty foundation had long since ceased to wave in the air of the morning of the world. When the first stone was laid in the construction of the first of Egypt's pyramids, the tree had been dead a thousand generations.

And yet, in spite of the tree's great age — and here is the mystery — in the petrified trunk of the root is a great gash cut, according to the best modern judgments, by axes of sharpened steel.

And what does this imply? It implies a civilization superior to that of Egypt and immeasurably more ancient. It implies that a vast page from history, and from the childhood of the race, has been forgotten. And it intimates that a civilization existed on the American continent ages before the mound-builders erected their open-air altars, and centuries before the copper behind the pictured rocks of Lake Superior was mined by a race long since extinct.

There is no chance of mistake about this find, for the circumstances that surround it remove all chance of error or opportunity for trickery. Theodore S. Solomon, for whom Solomon City, near Nome, was named, with dozens of his men can testify to the finding of the great stump buried in the earth, at the depth of a hundred feet. And hundreds of people from Nome visited it before it was entirely excavated from the tons of rock, earth, and coal that lay over it. The find was made on Candle Creek, Alaska, at the bottom of the Solomon Mines. Had it been a couple of feet lower it would never have been found, as the mine had gone to its greatest depth when the topmost portions of the find were unearthed.

The gashes show the grain of the wood and indicate that the axe which did the cutting was extremely sharp. The tree fell through age, but the axe work was apparently done either for the sap or to blaze a trail through the dense and dangerous prehistoric woods. But there are many questions which American scientists have yet to decide concerning this find. This exhibit will occupy a central portion of the Alaska building at the Alaska-Yukon-Pacific Exposition, and by the time the 1909 exposition opens, it is hoped science will have come to some conclusion in regard to this find.

Many ancient relics discovered in the North could hint at civilizations long forgotten. One expedition in the 1920s, however, apparently found what archaeologists had only dreamed of discovering — the ancient inhabitants themselves. This story appeared in the Daily Alaskan on March 18, 1920.

Lost Tribe of the Arctic

Hidden for centuries under the ice fields of Alaska, a scientific expedition discovered the remains of an unknown prehistoric arctic race.

This remarkable find of an unknown race includes the fully clothed remains of one hundred individuals who apparently met sudden death in a village of six huts, afterward covered by ice and snow, where they remained sealed until the present time.

The life, habits, and physical appearance of this tribe bore little resemblance to the Eskimos.

The discovery was made near Point Barrow, the northernmost tip of Alaska. Dr. Van Valin, head of the expedition, was sent out two and a half years ago by the University of Pennsylvania to make an exhaustive study of the Eskimos.

He was investigating a shallow swale in search of Eskimo relics when his attention was attracted by the peculiar character of some debris. This led to a still further examination. Buried beneath four feet of ice, snow, and tundra were uncovered what was recognized at once as the wreckage of a collection of ancient huts. They had been constructed of driftwoods of various kinds, covered by dome-shaped roofs cut from the tundra. The roofs had long since fallen in, while little remains even of the sides of the huts.

The great discovery, however, was made when the explorers came upon the first of the frozen bodies. In many instances the positions of the bodies, all in a perfect state of preservation, frozen in solid blocks of ice, suggested that death had overtaken them unexpectedly. Some had died in the act of drinking; at least, that is the supposition from the presence in their hands of what appeared to be long tubes, one end of which was held between the lips.

Of the hundred or more bodies, nearly all were fully attired. Many were lying on beds, covered by polar bear skins. The apparel worn by some showed that the race had learned to fabricate clothing from the skins of birds and that they also understood the art of tanning or curing skins of animals.

One thing seems certain. The community was overtaken by some suddenly developing catastrophe. Included among the bodies found in a perfect state of preservation were men, women, and children of all ages. The clothing, furs, and skins were in perfect condition. Exposure to the air, however, quickly caused much of it to disintegrate. As a result but few specimens of the clothing are included in the collection brought back by Mr. Van Valin.

Unfortunately, the fate which befell the skins and furs and bird-skin suits awaited the wearers as well. Although when discovered many of the bodies still retained their flesh, there was no means at the command of Dr. Van Valin for preserving them. But a few hours' exposure to warmer air was required to cause the fleshy portions to sluff away. Fortunately, however, the skeletons remain intact, perfectly articulated, and within a very short time will be in the university museum.

Many interesting relics were discovered in the ruins, including pieces of pottery.

Inquiries by Dr. Van Valin among the Eskimos proved that they had no traditions connected with the ancient inhabitants whose remains he had discovered.

Giants of the Past

During the Pleistocene Epoch, great herds of mastodons and mammoths roamed North America and Asia. According to scientists, these ancient elephants became extinct between 4,000 and 10,000 years ago. Hundreds of fossils of their bones and tusks have been discovered, especially in the wilderness of the North Country. According to some reports, whole mammoths have been found frozen in glacial ice.

But that's not all. In 1881, Native residents of the Yukon Territory reported seeing mammoths in the upper Stikine River area. The Copper River people of Interior Alaska described encounters with "huge, woolly beasts with horns like the trunks of birch trees," and said that in the winter, "puffs of steam issue from their nostrils like the escape pipe of a steamboat." Did small numbers of the shaggy beasts survive in Alaska and the Yukon until relatively modern times?

Cola F. Fowler, the author of this account, went to Alaska in 1877 as an agent for the Alaska Fur and Commercial Company. He spent the next twelve years in Interior Alaska, buying and trading for furs and fossil ivory. His story was published by the Philadelphia Press *on May 5, 1889, and reprinted by the* (Sitka) Alaskan *on June 22, 1889.*

The Mastodon Hunters

Two years ago last summer, I left Kodiak for a trip to the headwaters of the Snake River, where our traveling agents had established a trading station at an Indian village. The chief of this family of Inuits was named To-lee-ti-ma and to him I was well recommended. He received me hospitably, and I at once began to negotiate for a big lot of fossil ivory which his tribe had cached near the village. The lot weighed several thousand pounds and consisted of the principal and the inferior tusks of mammoths, the remains of thousands of which gigantic animals are to be found in the beds of Interior Alaska water courses.

I subjected the ivory to a rigid inspection, and upon two of the largest tusks, I found fresh blood traces and decomposed flesh.

I questioned To-lee-ti-ma, and he assured me that less than three months before a party of the young men had encountered a drove of the monsters about fifty miles above where he was then encamped, and had succeeded in killing two, an old bull and a cow.

At my request he sent for the leader of the hunting party, a young and intelligent Indian, and I questioned him closely about his adventure among a race of animals that the scientific people claim are extinct. He told me a straightforward story, and I have no reason to doubt its truth.

He and his band were searching along a dry water course for ivory and had found a considerable quantity. One of the Indians who was in advance rushed in upon the main body one morning with the startling intelligence that, at a spring of water about a mile from where they then were, he had discovered "signs" of several of the "big teeth." They had come down to the spring from a lofty plateau farther inland and had fed in the vicinity of the water for some time.

The chief immediately called about him his hunters and started for the spring. They had nearly reached it when they heard loud, shrill, trumpet-like calls, and an enormous creature came crashing toward them through the brush, the ground trembling under his footfalls. With wild cries of terror, the Indians fled, except for the chief and the scout who first discovered the trail of the monsters. They were armed with large-caliber muskets and stood their ground, opening fire on the mammoth. A bullet must have penetrated the creature's brain for he staggered forward and fell dead, and subsequently, on their way back to their camp, they overhauled a cow "big teeth" which was evidently the mate of the first one killed.

I asked the hunter to describe the monster and,

taking a sharp stick, he drew me a picture of the male animal in the soft clay. According to his description, it was at least twenty feet in height and thirty feet in length. In general shape it was not unlike an elephant, but the ears were smaller, its eyes bigger, its trunk longer and more slender. Its tusks were yellowish-white in color and six in number. Four of these tusks were like a boar, one on either side of each jaw; they were about four feet long and came to a sharp point. The other two tusks he brought away. I measured them and they were over fifteen feet in length and weighed upwards of 250 pounds each. They gradually tapered to a sharp point and tapered inward. The monster's body was covered with long, coarse hair of a reddish dun color. I took a copy of the rude sketch made by the Indian, and you are welcome to reproduce it in the press.

By the way, our late governor, the Hon. Alfred P. Swineford, has pretty carefully investigated the matter, and he is certain from a thorough sifting of Native testimony that large herds of these monsters are to be found on the plateaus in Interior Alaska about the headwaters of the Snake River.

The crude sketch made by the Native hunter seems to have depicted an animal that resembled a "four tusker," an ancient elephant that lived during the Miocene Age. Yet in the 1890s all pictures of mastodons showed an animal with two long, curling tusks. The "four tusker" was unknown to science at that time.

In their account of finding a tropical valley high in the mountains of the arctic, Hank Russell and Jack Lee told of finding huge footprints that could only have been created by a mammoth or mastodon. They were not the only ones to report discovering such tracks. Dr. J. P. Frizzel's find on Unimak Island in the Aleutian Chain gave more evidence of the existence of living mammoths. This account appeared in the Nome Semi-Weekly News *on September 29, 1903, headlined "Finds Tracks of Mammoth." Dr. Frizzel gave the following brief statement.*

Tracks of the Mammoth

I do not wish to make myself ridiculous to the scientific world by stating as a fact that at least one living specimen of the mammoth family is still roaming at large on the American side in the far arctic regions. However, I saw, with my own eyes, comparatively fresh tracks that apparently could not have been made by any other kind of animal but a mammoth. I ran across the animal's tracks on the island of Unimak, which is 125 miles around and twenty-six miles in width. It is about four miles from the mainland, and animals can walk back and forth from the island.

The tracks could be distinctly seen in the ice and snow, and I followed them for quite a distance. They sank four inches into the hard, frozen ground. They were four feet apart, showing that distance to be the stride of the animal. The width of the tracks was nineteen by twenty inches. In each track was the distinct impression of eighteen toes.

While removing the frozen overburden to uncover gold-bearing gravel, miners often found the skeletal remains and body parts of Pleistocene animals. Unfortunately, many of these discoveries were lost to science, as the miners had no way to preserve the bodies. However, one mammoth, found frozen in the ice in Siberia, was recovered by scientists and successfully preserved. The Nome Nugget *published this story on December 12, 1903.*

Frozen in Time

In northeastern Siberia, just beyond the limits of the concession owned by the Northeast Siberian Company, the only perfect specimen of a mammoth was found last spring and was conveyed to St. Petersburg, where it is now on exhibition at the Museum of the Imperial Academy of Sciences.

The mammoth was found virtually intact, preserved by natural cold storage just as he died a hundred thousand or more years ago in the wilds of Siberia.

This is the only specimen that is complete, with eyes, tongue, hair, skin, and all the most perishable parts. Only a portion of one tusk was missing when the body was found. How perfect the body was is indicated by the fact that the stomach was filled with food in various stages of digestion.

Many other mammoths have been discovered in Siberia more or less complete, and with much of the flesh in an excellent state of preservation, but some important parts have always been missing. As a rule, the animals and local residents had devoured a large part of the flesh before scientists could reach the body.

In this case the czar's government placed every resource, including the army, at the disposal of the scientists.

The bones have been taken out of the mammoth, mounted, and placed on exhibition. The skin, with the tusks and eyes, has been mounted and placed in a thoroughly lifelike position alongside the skeleton.

The tongue, which is nineteen inches long, the intestines, and other internal organs of the mammoth are kept in great jars of alcohol close at hand.

This mammoth was first reported by a Cossack named Jawlowsky. He found it in a glacier near the Beresowka River, a tributary of the Kolyma River, in far northeastern Siberia. The nearest settlement is Srednekolymsk, about 600 miles away.

The situation of the body was a very extraordinary one. It lay in an enormous pocket of ice, between the mountains, near the riverbank. The ice was evidently the relic of the great glacier that existed there in former ages. The upper ice in time flowed away, leaving only the lower part shut up in this pocket.

A slight melting of the surface of the ice left a bright, smooth space, peering through which the Cossack Jawlowsky saw the ancient mammoth preserved, as we sometimes see a lobster in a cake of ice. The Cossack knew how interesting such relics were to civilized men and promptly reported this one.

Through the agency of Mr. Horn, the chief of

police of Kolymsk, the Cossack's report was conveyed to the governor of Yakutsk. He, being interested in scientific matters, promptly communicated the report to the Imperial Academy of Sciences at St. Petersburg. An expedition was organized by the academy to recover the body of the mammoth. Dr. Otto Herz, curator of the Imperial Museum, was appointed leader of the group.

The expedition proceeded along the Trans-Siberian Railroad as far as Irkutsk. From there to the place of the discovery is a journey of fully 3,000 miles. The scientists made part of this journey in boats down the Lena River to Yakutsk. Then they started on a tremendous overland journey to Sredne-kolymsk. They took five horses for transport. The government gave them a company of Cossacks for transport. A large part of the way lay through virgin forest. Then came the formation called the taiga, a sort of arctic moorland, which becomes swampy and dangerous in summer.

The scientists had to live on salt fish, mare's milk, and stewed tree bark. Several lives were lost on the journey, but the scientists reached their destination.

When the scientists arrived in the vicinity of the mammoth, they were unable to locate it because they were not sure of the exact location in reference to the site marked on the map.

"We were at a loss to proceed further, for the maps of the district are not detailed, and we found ourselves in the midst of a vast number of exactly similar ice mounds. Finally, however, my nostrils detected a strange odor, the flesh of the monster which had become uncovered and was decomposing. By dint of walking in the direction whence the smell seemed to come, I finally located the grave. In my excitement I ran the last mile of the way against the fast-increasing stench. At the grave I found a faithful Cossack, who, for fifty days, had stood guard over the carcass at the command of his superior officer. He had covered it over with dry soil to a depth of three feet, but even through this protection the smell made its way."

Dr. Herz then describes the long hair and thickness of hide of the mammoth and how the stomach was found full of undigested food. The attitude in which he was found shows that he met his death by slipping on a slope, for his rear legs are bent up so that it would be impossible for him to raise himself. Dr. Herz writes:

"The impromptu grave into which the animal plunged was made of sand and clay, and his fall probably caused masses of neighboring soil to loosen and cover him completely. This happened in the late autumn or at the beginning of winter, to judge by the vegetable matter found in the stomach; at any rate, shortly afterward the grave became flooded, ice following. This completed the cold storage, still further augmented by vast accumulations of soil all round — a shell of ice hundreds of feet thick, enclosed by yards upon yards of soil that remain frozen for the greater part of the year. Thus the enormous carcass was preserved for how long no one knows, through hundreds of centuries perhaps, until not so many years ago some movement of the earth spat forth the fossil mausoleum, leaving it exposed to sun and wind, until gradually, very gradually, the ice crust wore off and revealed to the passing Cossack the long-hidden treasure."

The flesh was treated with arsenic and then sewn

up in raw cowhide, which shrinks, becomes airtight, and preserves the contents.

The veins of the mammoth were still full of coagulated blood, just as they were left when the animal was killed by suffocation. This condition was one of the indications which showed the scientists the way in which the deceased met his end. The mammoth was a young male not over thirty years old. In the teeth were found pieces of the beast's last meal.

The mammoth was so complete that even his tail was in perfect condition. It was a huge affair, with a tuft of hair at the end. The stomach of the mammoth was covered with long reddish hair similar to that of the modern yak bull. . . . This hair is fourteen inches long.

Dr. Herz transported the mammoth's remains overland, by sledges, to Irkutsk. Thence they were carried by the Trans-Siberian Railroad to European Russia.

One of the most bizarre stories ever to come out of the Northland was that of Reverend Sheldon Jackson's discovery of mastodon remains. Rev. Jackson was a well-known missionary and the founder of Sheldon Jackson College in Sitka. He claimed to have made the discovery somewhere in Interior Alaska; the Kazatka Lake he mentions is no longer found on maps, and may have dried up or been renamed. Here is Rev. Jackson's account as it appeared in the Alaska Searchlight *on February 12, 1898.*

Entombed in a Glacier

Five years ago I started on a journey from our mission house on the lower Yukon, intending to be absent five months, visiting all the missionary stations under the Arctic Circle. I was accompanied on this journey by three Eskimos and six of the best dogs in the mission, harnessed to sledges. . . . We had traveled 2,000 miles northeasterly, making our last stopping place Kazatka Lake, a body of water thirty miles long and twenty miles wide, with rugged mountains on either side, and a flat and marshy valley at either end, with a river flowing in from the north and another river flowing out from the south. At the intersection of mountain and river there were glaciers common to the whole country, but these possessed peculiarities that alone belonged to them. They were dead glaciers, by reason of having lost their means of locomotion.

There is nothing as noisy as a live, moving glacier

— nothing so dead and silent as the glacier that has lost its legs. But there were legs imbedded in the ice; they were there by the hundreds and I may truly say by the thousands and were attached to huge animals, the mastodons or "elephants of the arctic," still perfect in form, some standing, others sitting on their haunches, with large trunks hanging between massive ivory tusks. They were caught in the embrace of the deadly foe, which preserved them as freshly as though they had been imprisoned but yesterday.

Taking a knife from my belt, I slashed a piece of meat and gave it to the dogs, and they ate it as ravenously as though sliced from a quarter of a moose.

In the 1880s and 1890s several papers reported mastodon sightings. This account is unique because it is the only known report of live mammoths in southern Canada. The encounter probably occurred along the upper reaches of the Stikine River. At that time, much of the area was unexplored, and it remains a wilderness today. This story first appeared in the Juneau Free Press and was reprinted in the (Sitka) Alaskan on March 4, 1893.

The Hunter's Story

The following is copied from an exchange received by the last mail from the *Juneau Free Press*, which paper passed out of existence some two years ago.

The Stikine Indians positively assert that within the last five years they have frequently seen animals which, from the description given, must be mastodons.

Last spring, while out hunting, one of their hunters came across a series of large tracks, each the size of the bottom of a salt barrel, sunk deep in the moss. He followed the curious trail for some miles, finally coming out in full view of his game. As a class these Indians are the bravest of hunters, but the proportions of this new species of game filled the hunter with terror, and he took to swift and immediate flight.

He describes the creature as being as large as a post trader's store, with great, shining, yellowish-white tusks and a mouth large enough to swallow a man at a single nip. He further states that the animal was undoubtedly of the same kind as those whose bones and tusks lie all over the country.

The fact that other hunters have told of seeing these monsters browsing on the herbs up along the river gives a certain probability to the story. Over on Fortymile Creek, bones of mastodons are quite plentiful. One ivory tusk nine feet long projects from one of the sand dunes on the creek, and single teeth have been found that are so large that they would have been a good load for a man to carry.

I believe that the mule-footed hog still exists, that live mastodons play tag with the aurora every night on Fortymile Creek in Alaska.

In October of 1899, McClure's Magazine published a story titled "The Killing of the Mammoth." It was probably the most controversial story ever to appear in that publication. The magazine was besieged by mail. Some readers dubbed it "The Great Mammoth Hoax." Others hailed the account as the landmark event of that century, while still others were outraged by the killing of the animal. Here's the full story, as written by Henry Tukeman.

Killing of the Mammoth

In 1890, I journeyed, by way of St. Michaels and the Yukon River, to Alaska. The Klondike had not then been discovered, and the Alaska Commercial Company's steamer failing to get further than Fort Yukon, owing to the lateness of the season, it was at this point I found myself when winter set in. A small tribe of Indians live at Fort Yukon. I listened to many an interesting yarn from the old tribesmen over the long winter

One night I had opened some old 'Graphics for the benefit of "Joe" — an ancient head-man in the tribe. Turning the page, we came to the picture of an elephant, whereupon old Joe became very excited, and finally explained to me, with some reluctance, that he had seen one of these animals "up there," indicating the north with his hand. Nor could any denial of mine that any such animals existed on this continent shake him.

To humor the old fellow, I asked him to tell me

the tale, which he did after much persuasion.

"Once, many summers ago, me and Soon-thai, we go up the Porcupine River — Soon-thai is my son; he is dead now. By and by, we leave the river and go up a little river many days, to the mountain. But the mountain is too steep and very high, and we cannot climb up it. We go back a little way, and we shoot a moose at the mouth of a little gully. Soon-thai, he goes off and he finds the gully ends in a little cliff, and he climbs up it and finds a cave. He is brave — he goes in the cave, and at the end is a small hole, and Soon-thai looks through it and sees an easy way to climb up the mountain. By and by, we take some meat and we go through the cave, and it is full of big bones, bigger than my body, and I am afraid; but we go through the little hole into the sunlight, and I have courage, and we climb to the top of the mountain.

"Soon-thai says, 'We shoot plenty beaver in the valley, eh?' I say, 'No, that is the Devil's country,' and I tell him it is the country called in Indian Tee-Kai-Koa ('the Devil's footprint'). Then Soon-thai, he is a little afraid, but by and by he says, 'Come, my father, we will not stay long; in two days we will shoot plenty beaver and then we will run back.'

"After two days, we make a raft and cross a long lake, like a river, and the next day we see Tee-Kai-Koa!"

The old man rose and pointed before him. A strange glitter was in his eye, and the beads of perspiration stood out on his forehead. I could not doubt for a moment that he was describing what he had really seen.

"He is throwing water over himself with his long nose, and his two teeth stand out before his head for ten gun-lengths, turned up and shining like a swan's wing in the sunlight. His hair is black and long, and hangs down his sides like driftwood from the tree branches after the floods, and this cabin beside him would be as a two-week-old bear cub beside its mother. We do not speak, Soon-thai and I, but we look and look, and the water he throws over his back runs in little rivers down his sides. Presently he lies down in the water, and the waves come through the reeds up to our armpits, so great is the splash. Then he gets up and shakes himself, and all is a mist like a rainstorm round him.

"Suddenly Soon-thai throws up his gun, and before I can stop him, he fires — boom! — at Tee-Kai-Koa. Ah, the noise! It is a cry like a thousand geese, only shriller and louder, and it fills the valley till it reaches to the mountains, and all the world seems to have nothing in it but that angry cry. As the gun smoke rises above the reeds, Tee-Kai-Koa sees it and begins to run through the water toward it, and the noise of his splashing is as of all the wild fowl in the world rising from a calm lake at sunset.

"We turn and run, Soon-thai and I. We run through the trees away from our camp, for it is toward it Tee-Kai-Koa has gone, chasing the smoke, and after we have run a long distance, we rest and listen. But again we hear the great cry of Tee-Kai-Koa as he seeks us, and we have a new strength in our legs to run on and on."

The old Indian sat down and wiped his hand over his forehead, and for fully ten minutes no word was spoken — he perhaps thinking of his dead son, I racking my brains to remember what my school edition of Cuvier said about mammoths, for I had confirmed a wild idea that had flashed through my brain when the elephant's picture was first noticed. Presently the old man rose and stepped to the door of the cabin.

"Do not seek Tee-Kai-Koa, white man, lest you have no tale to tell us as I have told you." And he stepped out into the clear, frosty night, leaving me to wonder how he had divined my thoughts so accurately. . . .

In the tribe of Indians wintering at Fort Yukon was an active, intelligent young fellow named Paul, who spoke English well and was always in demand during the summer months as a pilot on the steamers of the A. C. Company. Paul had a strain of Scotch blood in his veins, and I found, after becoming intimate with him, that he had as much curiosity as I had about Tee-Kai-Koa and a profound contempt for the superstition of its being a "devil."

When I told Paul of some elephant-shooting experiences of mine in Africa in the '70s, he was eager to go off together during the coming summer and bag the mammoth, if he really was there. . . .

We bid goodbye to Fort Yukon on a fine morning early in July, poling our way up the Porcupine River in a long, narrow polingboat which we had built for the purpose.

On August 2 — my birthday, I recollected — we cached our stuff, pushing on to look at our route and have a peep at the "Devil's country". . . .

Climbing to the ledge, we found the cave, or tunnel, as it more properly was. It was about 200 feet long and wide enough for three men to walk abreast. The entire length was literally paved with gigantic mammoth bones, which made even the matter-of-fact Paul exclaim. I experimented on a piece of spinal vertebrae and was glad to find that the solid bullet of my .303 drilled through them with ease. . . .

I will not detail the weary work of the portage from the "little river." We had to use our blocks and tackle to land our stuff at the tunnel entrance. Finally we had everything at the summit, and a few days later, on the banks of the Tee-Kai-Koa River.

As for Paul, I have never met his equal in any of my travels. He was strong, active, untiring, cheerful, and full of the Native ingenuity which overcame obstacles as soon as they appeared, while his courage, and his quiet and absolute confidence in our ultimate success, acted as a nerve tonic to me when I found myself speculating whether we had too heavy an undertaking on hand.

On August 29, we had our first sight of the mammoth. There he stood in a little clearing, the great beast that only one other living man had seen, tearing up great masses of lichenous moss and feeding as an elephant feeds. . . . It is idle for me to describe him closely, and I need only speak of the feeling of awe inspired by the sight of this stupendous beast, quietly feeding in oblivion of the two pygmies who were planning his destruction. . . .

About twenty-five miles below our first camp we had found a clump of spruce trees larger than any we had seen in the valley, and here we set to work. At one side of the two largest trees, and across a small dry watercourse, we built a solid erection of five rounds of logs and placed within this a mass of dry and rotten wood, leaving one small hole where we could crawl in and light it. On top we felled the nearest large trees. When the structure was completed, it looked like a huge drift-pile of green logs.

We put ladder pegs up to the branches of the

two highest standing trees about sixty feet up, and selecting suitable places, built seats and took up rope with which we could lash ourselves in if necessary. By September we had everything prepared, and we had but to prove the truth of my supposition — that smoke would attract our quarry. . . .

By the sixteenth, everything was ready, and before daylight we placed our rifles and cartridges in our stations in the trees. We then started out, and by 10 a.m. had located our quarry, about three miles away. He seemed to be restless and kept sniffing the air. A very quiet breeze was blowing in the treetops.

We fired an armful of dry wood and started back as fast as we could run, but the moment the smoke rose that terrible cry came booming down the valley behind us, and we felt the earth vibrate as the mammoth charged in our direction. We knew it was a veritable race for life as we tore through the woods, touching off the prepared fires with a match as we passed.

At last we came to the log pile, and in a few seconds a thin wreath of smoke announced that the battle would soon begin. We hastened to our stations. We were not kept in suspense long. Rushing forth from the forest and charging up to the woodpile with an ear-splitting cry, the king of the primeval forests stood beneath us in all his pride of strength.

He was evidently puzzled for a moment by the huge log pile confronting him, through which the smoke was now rolling in a thick volume. But with the crack of our rifles came the most appalling scream of rage I have ever head, and the vast brute, apparently unaffected by our shots, attacked the woodpile with incredible fury. Charging his enormous tusks beneath it, he gave a mighty heave, and for a second lifted the whole mass of green logs — remember they were pinned together and stood at least twenty-five feet high — clear off the ground. Finding this more than even his colossal strength could compass, he seized a top timber, a solid green log twenty-five feet long and over a foot in diameter, and threw it clear behind him.

Meanwhile our rifles had not been idle, and I had already got through my second magazine-full, generally aiming behind the ear. So loud was the noise, scream following scream till the hills rang with the sound, that I could not hear the report of my rifle, but the barrel, hot in my hand, told me that the wicked little bullets were speeding on their mission.

The mammoth seemed to have no idea that his assailants were above him, but blindly attacked the burning woodpile, seizing the logs and hurling them this way and that, till I saw it was only a matter of minutes until the whole edifice should be scattered far and wide. One log, smaller than the rest, came hurling through the air into my refuge and crashed through the branches overhead. Another struck the tree about halfway up, splintering the bark and nearly shaking me off my seat.

But the end was drawing near, for the great brute was bleeding profusely from the mouth and ears, and staggered uncertainly back and forth. A feeling of pity and shame crept over me as I watched the failing strength of this mighty prehistoric monarch whom I had outwitted and despoiled of a thousand peaceful years of harmless existence. It was as though we were robbing nature and Old Mother

Earth herself of a child born to her younger days, in the dawn of time. . . .

The deed was done, and we now had to justify it by saving the skin, bones, and every portion capable of preservation. This proved a tremendous task. . . . By the middle of December, the bones were all removed from the body, carefully cleaned, and numbered. When once we had the hide safely away, we were able to light a large fire and roast a lot of the meat. I took careful measurements of the lungs, heart, and all the perishable portions.

We worked steadily till nearly the end of January, not leaving the camp at all. The meat was not unpalatable, but terribly tough. We buried the best portions in the ever-frozen ground and were thus able to preserve it perfectly. . . .

Finally we built a solid cache of heavy green logs in a safe place, and having shut everything securely in it, we built a small boat and waited for the opening of the river.

We journeyed down the Tee-Kai-Koa River to the Chandalar, and thence to the Yukon and St. Michaels, and proceeded by the first steamer to San Francisco. There I met a Mr. Conradi — quite by accident — and finding him deeply interested in zoology, I disclosed the secret of the prize we had left on the banks of the Tee-Kai-Koa.

I had kept the matter secret because I wished to find out for myself from the various authorities in America and Europe something as to the value of the mammoth. My design was, if possible, to get the British Museum authorities to purchase it. Mr. Conradi's offer astounded me — it was in millions of dollars — and after a week's thought I closed with him.

Paul absolutely refused to accept more than a quarter-share, arguing, not without reason, that even this portion was more than he knew what to do with or could possibly spend. Civilization had few attractions for him; he soon tired of 'Frisco and used to long impatiently for the wilds.

Paul and I went north that summer, and wintered on the Tee-Kai-Koa River near our cache. In the spring, we conveyed the mammoth to a certain place on the Yukon River, where we met Mr. Conradi, and everything was packed in specially prepared cases. . . .

I believe that the most generally accepted theory heretofore has been that Mr. Conradi found the carcass frozen in an iceberg in the Arctic Ocean. The measurements, exactly as taken by me, were handed to the Smithsonian and accepted without question as his own.

Was the story of "The Killing of the Mammoth" really a fabrication, or did Tukeman fictionalize an actual killing of the great beast? The solution to this and other mysteries of the Northland may never be discovered.

Index

A

Alaska 9, 16, 23, 35, 47, 58, 61,
  74, 85, 92, 100, 107, 108,
  123, 129, 133, 134, 146,
  147
Alaska Commercial Company
  147, 150
Alaska Fur and Commercial
  Company 134
Alaska Life magazine 23, 26
Alaska Mining Record 97
Alaska Peninsula 74
Alaska Searchlight 143
Alaska Weekly 48, 51, 58, 87,
  94, 99, 103
Alaska-Yukon Magazine 16, 38,
  81, 126
Alaska-Yukon-Pacific Exposition
  126, 128
Alaska-Yukon Pioneers 9, 92, 94
Alaskan 36, 72, 134, 145
Ancient artifacts 10, 115,
  118–119, 120, 122 123,
  124–125, 127
Anvil Creek 81, 83
Arctanger, John 68, 73
Arctic Ocean 79
Austin, Ned 20

B

Baccus, Judge 113
Badlam, Alexander 116
Baranof, Alexander 68
Barkdull, Calvin 9, 94–96
Barwell, C. S. W. 125
Bering Sea 23
Black Hills 88
Blackburn, William 63
Blankenship, H. O. 78–80
Bonanza Creek 124–125
Borusof, Paul 73
Bouikof, Colonel 73
Bowie, Colonel J. C. 61
British Columbia (B.C.) 15, 53,
  85
Brooks, W. M. 61

C

Candle Creek 78, 80, 126-127
Cape Fanshaw 95

Cape Prince of Wales 78, 79
Cape Yakataga 92
Cassiar Mountains 50, 51
Chandalar River 154
Chatham Straits 32
Coal Creek 63
Cody, Albert 61
Cold Bay 74, 77
Conrad, William 122
Copper River 35, 43, 133
Cordova Daily News 43
Corson, Dr. H. R. 36
Craig, R. J. 20
Crescent Lake 94-96
Cross Sound 92
Culver, Fred 97

D

Daily Alaska Dispatch 107
Daily Alaskan 61, 129
Daily Klondike Nugget 63
Dawson City 120, 124
Dawson Indians 35
Dewey Creek 122
Douglas City 28
Douglas Island News 122
Dutch Harbor 74, 75, 77

E

Eliza Anderson, The 74-77
Eskimos 129
Etolin, Adolph 73

F

Fairbanks 107
Feodorovna, Princess Olga 73
Fort Nelson River 50
Fort Wrangell 99, 100
Fort Yukon 147, 150
Fortymile Creek 146
Fowler, Cola F. 134–136
Frederick Sound 95
French, Allison 107
Frizzel, Dr. J. P. 137

G

Gastineau Channel 28
Ghosts 67, 68, 72, 74, 76, 77, 79,
  82, 86, 87, 112–113
Goodhope Bay 78
Gowen, Sam 94

Index

Greenslate, Jim 94
Grimm, Frank 81
Gulf of Alaska 74, 75

H
Hall, George T. 61
Hanson, Captain A. C. 61
Herz, Dr. Otto 140–143
Hieroglyphics 120
Holden, William 63
Howard, Frank 16-18
Hudson Bay Company 97
Hydah Indians 38-40

I
Imperial Academy of Sciences
 138, 140

J
Jackson, Reverend Sheldon
 9, 143-144
Johansen, Knygg 23-25
John, Father 113
Juneau 85,86, 94, 116, 119
Juneau City Mining Record 28
Juneau Free Press 145

K
Keller, S. A. 28–31
Kershon, George 116–119
Kiwalik River 78, 80
Klondike 35, 64, 74, 88, 124, 147
Klondike Nugget 124
Kodiak Island 15, 58, 60, 134
Koo-Nok-Aa-Tee 36-37
Kugruk River 79

L
Lady in Blue, The 68
Lake Laberge 62
Lee, Jack 55, 57, 137
Lena River 140
*Lewis and Dryden's History of the
 Pacific Northwest* 74
Lewis, Captain 97
Liard River 50, 53
Little, James 99, 103
Longstreet, Mrs. C. S. 61
Lost mines 9, 91
 Gold 92, 95–96, 97, 104–
 106, 107–109, 111–113
 Mercury 101–102

Lost tribes 35, 38–39, 129–130

M
Mack, Don 85–86
Mackenzie River 107-109
Malaspina Glacier 16
Mammoths and mastodons 133
 Living 134–136, 137, 145, 147,
 148–150, 151, 152–154
 Remains 134, 138–142, 144,
 150
Manley, Horace Parker 111–113
McClure's Magazine 147
McLode brothers 10, 105–106
Mirages 58–60, 61-62
Mount Fairweather 62
Muir Glacier 62, 119
Murphy, Judge Thomas C. 110

N
Nagel, Mrs. 78
Nicodet, Henry 120
Nome 9, 78, 81, 122, 126, 127
Nome Nugget 78, 81, 85, 122,
 138
Nome Semi-Weekly News 137
North Pacific 74
North Pole 41
Northeast Siberian Company 138
Northwest Territories 107
Nushagak River 23

O
O'Brien, James 81, 83

P
Pathfinder 92
Perry, Frank 48-50, 51, 55, 57
Petrified forest 64–65
Petrified stump 126–127
Philadelphia Press 134
Pioneer Mining Company 9, 81,
 83
Porcupine River 107, 148
Powers, Captain 75–76
Powers, Ike 81
Prince of Wales Island 38
Princeton, B.C. 110

Index

R

Rampart 107
Ransmiller, J. N. 61
Reed, Frank 26-27
Richardson Highway 87
Romer, Charlie 87
Ross, Jack 28-29
Rowe, Captain J. E. 36
Russell, Hank 55-57, 137

S

San Francisco Examiner 116
Sasquatches 15, 16-18, 19–22
Scotte, Captain Sam C. 51-52, 57
Sea serpents 9, 15, 23, 24–25,
    26–27, 28–31, 32–33
Seattle Post Intelligencer 61, 74
Semi-Weekly World 110
Shamans 35, 36–37, 38-40
Sheldon Jackson College 143
Siberia 138-142
Similkameen River 110
Similkameen Star 110
Sitka 36, 68, 95, 98, 104, 143
Skagway 67, 86
Smith, Captain Tom 9, 32
Smithsonian Institution 126, 155
Snake River 134, 136
Snider, Percy 63-65
Solomon Mining Company
    10, 115, 126, 127
Solomon, Theodore S. 127
Sprague, A. J. 9, 32-33
Spray, Lafe 9, 81-84
Srednekolymsk 139, 140
St. Elias Mountains 16, 92
St. Michaels 58, 147, 154
St. Petersburg 138, 140
Stanford, Ole 92–93
Stanton, Dr. O. W. 9
Stikine River 51, 94, 104, 105,
    133, 145
Stroller's Weekly 32, 41, 104
Swineford, Gov. Alfred P. 136

T

Tagish Lake 85-86
Telegraph Creek 51
Thompson, C. L. 58
Tiekel City 87-89

Tiekel River 87
Tilbury, George 20
Tlingits 36, 38, 40, 92, 104
To-lee-ti-ma 134–136
Trans-Siberian Railroad 142
Tropical valleys 47, 48–50, 51-52,
    53–54, 55–57
Tukeman, Henry 147-155
Tulameen River 110-111
Turner, Bob 75
Tuxekan 38

U

Unimak Island 137
Unuk River 94

V

Valdez Miner 55, 57
Van Valin, Dr. 129–131
Vancouver, B. C. 110
Victoria Colonist 15, 19
Von Hasslocher, E. A. 38-40
Von Wrangel, Baron Ferdinand 73

W

Weizl, John 41-42
Whitehorse 85
Widrow, Mike 111–113
Wild Goose Railroad 82
Williams, Colonel J. Scott 53–54
Williams, Ethel 85–86
Willoughby, Dick 61
Wonders of Alaska, The 116
Woodchopper 63
Wrangell 9, 23, 94, 96, 99, 101,
    102, 105
Wrangell Sentinel 23, 53
Wright, Captain Tom 77
Wright, Reverend Arthur R. 43, 45

Y

Yakutat 16
Yakutat Indians 92
Yale, B.C. 19
Yukon 35, 53, 58, 61, 107, 124,
    133
Yukon River 63, 85, 92, 116–117,
    147, 154
Yvolnoff, Captain 41-42

About the Author

Ed Ferrell has lived in Alaska for almost fifty years. He spent much of his life teaching English in high schools throughout Southeast Alaska and has taught at the University of Alaska in Juneau. Ferrell devoted much of his free time to exploring Alaska's gold rush country and became interested in researching its past. His first books, *Biographies of Alaska-Yukon Pioneers*, Volumes 1 & 2, were published by Heritage Books. It was during his work on these volumes that Ferrell began collecting the newspaper accounts that have become *Strange Stories of Alaska and the Yukon*. Ferrell lives in Juneau, Alaska, with his wife, Nancy.

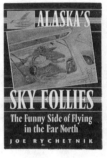